Cat Soup and Other Short Stories

by Jane Houng

QX PUBLISHING CO.

Cat Soup and Other Short Stories

Author: Jane Houng

Editor: Betty Wong

Illustrator: Stephanie Lin

Cover Designer: Oi Man Yeung

Published by:
QX PUBLISHING CO.
8/F, Eastern Central Plaza, 3 Yiu Hing Road, Shau Kei Wan, Hong Kong

Distributed by:
SUP Publishing Logistics (H.K.) Limited
3/F, C & C Building, 36 Ting Lai Road, Tai Po, N. T., Hong Kong

Printed by:
Elegance Printing & Book Binding Co., Ltd.,
Block A, 4/F, Hoi Bun Industrial Building, Hong Kong

Edition:
First edition, March 2016

ISBN 978 962 255 116 9

Printed in Hong Kong.

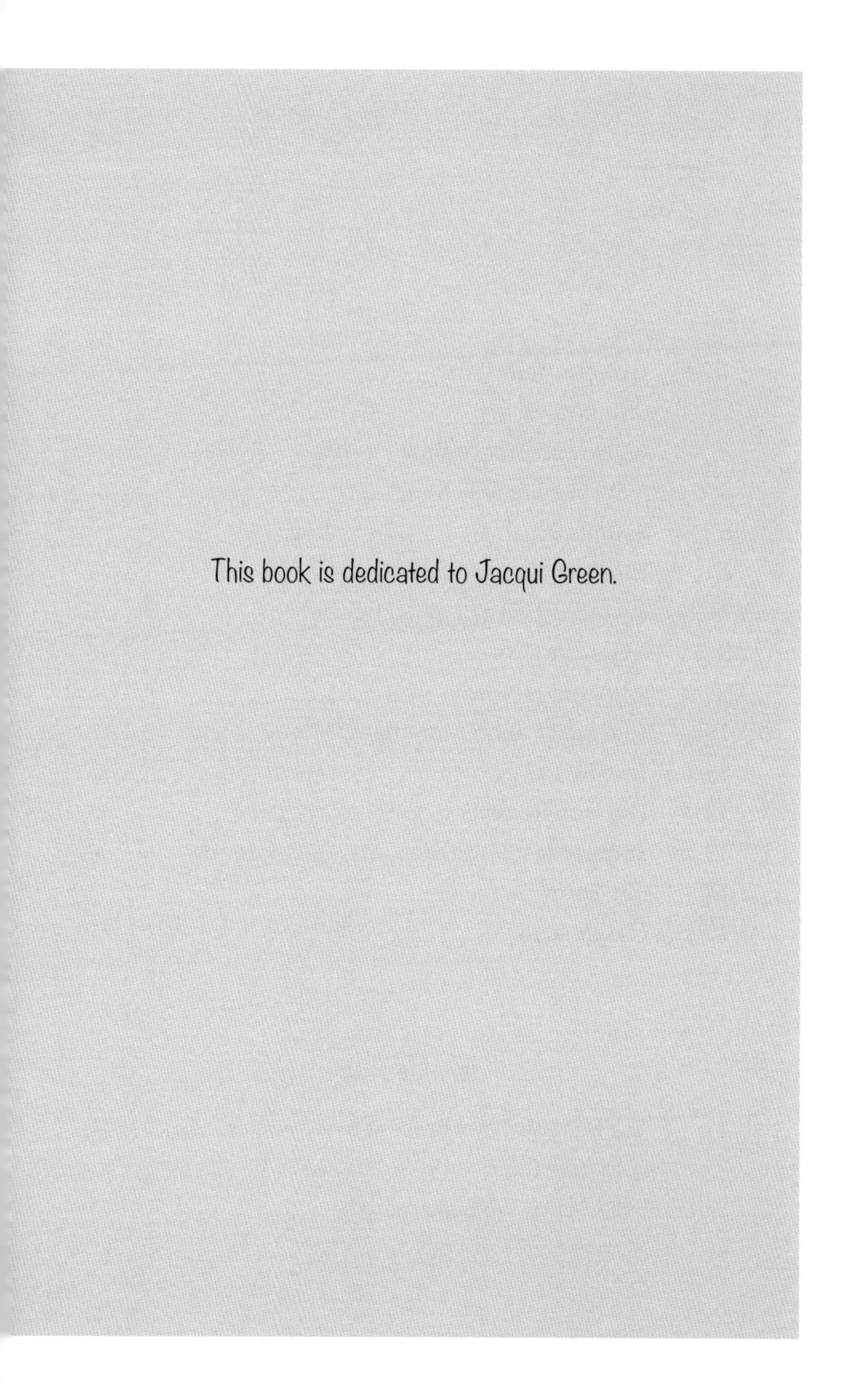

This book is dedicated to Jacqui Green.

Contents

Cat Soup

Twinkle Toes

Mooncake Magic: A Modern Chinese Fairy Tale

Cat Soup

Chapter 1
Typhoon Tam Tam

A strong wind blew down the mountain to the storm drain where Mama Mao and her two kittens lived. The rainwater was rising fast, swirling beneath their ledge like a raging river, splashing their whiskers. Two fat rats paddled by squeaking with fear.

'We're going to drown,' meowed Stolly, hiding his head in Mama Mao's warm fur.

Runty padded along the ledge to the broken gutter where they usually entered and exited. The wind whistled, rain poured, but the gap in the iron bars was clear of branches. *Surely they should escape,* he thought. *Run into the country park. Shelter under a bush.*

'Come back,' meowed Mama Mao.

A torch light shone above.

Runty tensed.

There were footsteps. Human footsteps. Coming closer.

Runty froze as a strong light flooded his sky. He couldn't see a thing.

Then the gutter shifted above him and fresh air gusted in.

Runty was about to run when something caught him. The something held him by his tail and lifted him out of the drain. 'Help, help!' he howled.

Mama Mao howled too.

Runty was dropped into a cage. A human face was looking at him. All lips and teeth. Runty recognised her. She was the girl who sometimes left them biscuits.

'He's so skinny,' she said.

What's she saying? thought Runty, and

hissed. He'd never been so close to a human before.

Another human face appeared. The girl's mama? She also had thin lips and snappy teeth. 'Let's go home now,' she said.

'But M-um, there's another one down there somewhere!' wailed June.

As the two humans walked away, the full force of the rain hit Runty's body.

There was more shifting and grating. Then Stolly, howling. Maybe the humans were trying to catch him too.

'This one has only half a tail,' said June.

Ouch! Something landed on top of Runty. Big brother Stolly! Never so happy to see him again, Runty nuzzled his neck.

'Where's Mama?' meowed Stolly.

From the storm drain came a yowling, and Mama Mao jumped out.

The two kittens watched as June tried to catch her, 'Over here, Mama!' they meowed.

When June tripped on a tree root, Mama Mao stopped and looked over her shoulder. She twitched her tail as if not sure which direction to run.

Then she ran towards the country park.

Chapter 2
Unfriendly Pets

Two moons waxed and waned. Runty and Stolly's new home was a laundry room on the third floor of a high-rise flat.

Squeezed behind a washing machine for safety, Stolly awoke from a cat nap. 'I dreamed of her again,' he meowed.

'Who?' Runty pretended to yawn.

'Mama.'

Runty stood up and stretched. 'She'll be fine.'

'I miss her,' said Stolly, reaching to rub noses.

Snubbing him, Runty strolled to the water dish in the middle of the room.

Lap, lap. His pink tongue was soon joined by Stolly's. So Runty rolled over to bite him. But Stolly wouldn't play.

Runty poked his tongue into his ear instead. An ear clean usually cheered his big brother up.

Footsteps. Human footsteps. In a panic, Stolly dashed back behind the washing machine.

'What a brave boy *you* are,' June said to Runty, who hadn't run away. She placed two bowls of biscuits beside the water dish.

Yum yum! Runty crunched a biscuit between his sharp teeth and allowed June to stroke him.

Stolly's tummy rumbled. How he longed to dig his nose into those delicious biscuits. *But hey!* Runty had finished one bowl and was eating from the other. 'Save some for me,' he meowed.

Runty kept eating!

Stolly stuck his nose out.

Holy cats! June was looking at him. Stolly backed up.

But June lunged forward and caught him by the scruff of his neck. 'I won't hurt you, you silly thing,' she said.

Stolly wriggled and spat as she pushed him into a cage. It was the one she'd used to catch them during typhoon Tam Tam.

Runty ran up to it and pressed his nose against the metal. Inside was a plate of Stolly's favourite fish, a bowl of water, a blanket, and a poop tray.

'Tell your brother I won't let him out until he stops spitting at me, okay?' said June, removing her rubber gloves.

Stolly hissed and spat.

'That's very rude,' said Runty.

'I want Mama,' Stolly howled.

'June is our mama now.'

'She doesn't smell nice.'

'But she feeds us, keeps us warm.'

Stolly clawed at the cage. 'She's not furry. She smells odd. I want my real mama.'

Night and day, he dreamed of how to escape.

Chapter 3

An Unwelcome Visitor

When Stolly finally learned some manners, the kittens were allowed the full run of the flat. One day, Runty was cleaning Stolly's face in the living room when the front door bell rang. The kittens scooted under the nearest cupboard.

'That must be Old Aunt Po,' called Mrs. Tam.

'*Ugh,* not her again!' June was in her bedroom practising Chinese characters for a dictation.

'Charity begins at home. Charity means being nice to neighbours,' said her mum.

'Even beggars?'

Mrs. Tam banged the flimsy hall wall. '*Especially* beggars. Anyway, collecting aluminium cans from rubbish bins is *not* begging.'

'Okay, okay.' June went back to her calligraphy.

Mrs. Tam opened the door and the kittens heard a new voice. They tracked two new flip-flopping feet. Dirty feet. Dirty curled toenails, which stopped a tail away from them.

Old Aunt Po sniffed. Sniffed again.

'Oh dear, do you have a cold?' asked Mrs. Tam.

'No, no,' said Old Aunt Po. 'I thought I could ... smell something.'

Oh dear. Had Stolly had a little accident again? Mrs. Tam couldn't *see* any evidence.

Runty poked his head out. The new voice had a scaly-snake face and straggly white hair. One black one sprouted from a mole on her chin. He hid his head, a second too late.

'Oh! You have a new cat,' cackled Old Aunt Po.

‘Two, actually. They’re kittens,’ replied Mrs. Tam, as Old Aunt Po sat down. ‘We rescued them during the typhoon last month. They’re a bit of a nuisance really. This flat is too small for two pets.’

‘Mum, I can hear you!’ shouted June from her bedroom.

The kittens tensed. What were the humans arguing about?

‘Bit of a nuisance, hey?’ repeated Old Aunt Po.

‘Well, sometimes they scratch our furniture,

and they run around here as if it's Happy Valley,' joked Mrs. Tam, going into the kitchen to boil some water.

Runty stole another look. *Uh-oh,* Old Aunt Po was looking directly at him! 'Come here, pussy pussy,' she whispered. *Pooh!* Her breath stank.

Mrs. Tam returned with a teapot and some dried plums. A sweet smell filled the air as she poured the tea.

Old Aunt Po slurped from her tea cup and chewed on a dried plum. 'If you don't mind me saying,' she said, between lip smacks, 'I think *one* cat is quite enough for a ten-year-old girl.'

'Well, they *are* brothers. It seems a shame to separate them,' said Mrs. Tam.

Old Aunt Po's cheeks cracked into hundreds of lines. 'Well, if you're ever going away and they need looking after, just call me.'

'Thank you. That may be useful,' said Mrs. Tam, and laughed.

Stolly cuddled closer to Runty. His brother's

fur felt comforting.

The moment Old Aunt Po left, June marched into the kitchen. 'Mum, please don't let her anywhere *near* my kittens.'

Mrs. Tam scraped half-chewed plums off Old Aunt Po's plate. 'She'd probably appreciate some extra cash,' she said.

Chapter 4
A Divinely Smelly Smell

On sunny days, Mrs. Tam opened the balcony doors to freshen up the flat. Stolly hadn't noticed that before. 'Come over here,' he called to his little brother, feeling the thrill of being outside. He carefully lowered a paw on to the tiles. They felt warm.

Runty ran straight past him to the railing. He squeezed his head between the bars and sniffed.

Stolly cautiously lowered another paw. The breeze ruffled his fur. *Drrr drrr. Tweet tweet.* The country park buzzed with cicadas, honey bees and birdsong. Stolly had forgotten how noisy nature was.

A bird hopped from branch to branch on a nearby tree. Runty crouched low.

Tweet, tweet. The bird flew away.

Stolly spotted another and licked his lips. He hadn't tasted bird since the days of the storm drain. His fat belly skimmed the tiles as he joined his brother at the railing. *Holy cats!* What a drop. He jumped back, bumping into something.

Crash! A plant pot smashed against the floor.

'Shh!' growled Runty.

Tweet, tweet. All the birds flew away.

'Sorry, brother.' Stolly sat on his haunches.

Runty settled beside him. *Who needs birds when there's salmon biscuits?* he thought. Below him was the public garden where, from June's bedroom window, he'd often watch her play. From the balcony, he could smell the bushes of the flower beds dancing in the wind.

Stolly traced the line of a fence that divided the garden from the country park. Running alongside the fence was the storm drain. His heart bumped. 'Hey, is that where we used to live?'

'You've only worked that out now?' Runty stood up and shook himself. There was a whirring sound from above. From a pulley, something large and square was travelling towards them.

Runty sniffed. What was that divinely smelly smell? He stepped forwards, looked upwards.

Great cats of fire! There was Old Aunt Po, on the balcony above, her bird's nest of hair swept back into a bun!

'Hello, little pussy pussies,' she cackled, easing the rope.

Stolly bolted behind the nearest plant pot.

The cage came to rest on the balcony floor. Runty balanced on his hind legs, lowered his front legs to the metal mesh. A fish hung from a hook inside. Its silver skin shone in the sunlight. Its dulled eyes looked crunchy. He pushed his tongue through the wire to try and lick it.

'A fresh fishy, for my little pussy pussies,' croaked Old Aunt Po.

'Keep away,' meowed Stolly.

But Runty stepped inside the cage.

At that moment, Old Aunt Po pulled the rope.

In a flash, Runty jumped out, almost getting his tail trapped.

Stolly raced back inside the flat.

As the cage lifted, it banged against the balcony railings, snapping its trapdoor shut.

The sound alerted June. 'Runty? Stolly? Where are you?' she called.

The cage swung upwards, faster and faster.

By the time June had reached the balcony, it had disappeared.

Chapter 5
Reunited

Fortunately for the kittens, Old Aunt Po's fish didn't visit at night.

From the balcony, the kittens sniffed the sweet evening air. It was heavy with the perfume of ginger flowers. Fireflies danced in the dark woods. Toads croaked. There were even a few stars twinkling above.

'I do *so* miss Mama,' meowed Stolly.

Runty settled on a mat to lick his coat clean. Now that he'd grown bigger there was a lot more of it to lick. How he appreciated June's daily brush. Not like his silly big brother, who'd race under the nearest cupboard whenever he heard June open the brush drawer.

Stolly sang a little song:

Runty and me,
The moon and the trees,
Mama I love you,
Where ever you be.

A cat yowled in the distance. Stolly and Runty pricked their ears.

The yowling grew louder, closer. It was the kind of yowl that humans throw shoes at.

Then there was the rustle of trampled leaves, the crack of broken branches.

Stolly's heart bumped.

A bush shook. Cat eyes flashed from under its leaves.

Stolly's heart jumped.

But Runty crept forward, poked his nose through the railing. A cat was running across the garden towards them. The cat was gazing upwards, as if looking for something. Her eyes glinted in the moonlight.

'Mama!' cried Runty.

'Runty!' cried Mama Mao.

'Mama!' cried Stolly.

'My boys!' meowed Mama Mao.

For a few seconds, their three little hearts beat as one.

The kittens asked their mama many questions about the Discovery Park Cat Clan, where she'd returned to. She told them she hunted butterflies, lizards and birds, usually at night. Daytimes, she'd sleep in an old pigsty under a papaya tree. She had many friends.

Stolly paced the balcony, thinking, wishing. If only he could jump the three floors down to the ground without hurting himself. 'I want to live in the country park with you, Mama!'

Mama Mao's whiskers drooped. 'You're much safer living up there,' she meowed. 'Here there are wild dogs. Hungry snakes. Other strange creatures.'

Almost on cue, there was a yowling from the darkness, the sound of squealing and skirmish.

Mama Mao arched her back and snarled. The kittens' tails bristled like bottle brushes.

'Come here, pussy pussy,' crooned a familiar voice.

Lit up by a lamppost, Old Aunt Po's ghostly face appeared. She had a hook of meat in one hand and a net bulging with animals in the other.

'Run, Mama!' cried Stolly as Old Aunt Po hobbled towards her.

Mama Mao turned tail and ran. 'I'll come again, I promise,' she called, before disappearing in the trees.

Chapter 6
The Great Escape

'I'm sorry. I couldn't wait,' meowed Stolly. Three nights had passed and Mama Mao hadn't returned as promised.

Runty looked down from the balcony railings: on the air-con one floor below was Stolly. His little tail wagged.

'Don't move, you idiocat,' Runty meowed.

'Stop insulting me. I'm not coming back.'

'Don't then.'

Oo-er! Stolly looked down and his tummy ached. The drop below yawned like a wild dog's mouth.

Runty wasn't scared of heights like his scaredy-cat brother. But there was only squeeze room for the two of them on the air-con. He'd have to risk it. Bunching his body into a ball, straightening his tail, he leapt. *Thud!*

'You could have flattened me,' grumbled Stolly.

'*You* could have lost one of your lives.'

'I just *have* to see Mama again.'

Runty tried to block his ears. *Rats and rattlesnakes,* Stolly's meows hit his pity nerve as usual. He looked up. There was no way they could jump back up to the flat. He studied the puzzle of pipes on the building wall. Using them to reach the ground was worth a try. Certainly better than sitting shoulder to shoulder with his whining brother.

'I know you can do it,' said Stolly.

Runty jumped down to the air-con shelf. 'Follow my lead. But whatever you do, don't look down.'

Stolly meows turned into wails. 'I'm not sure I can make it.'

'Well I'll go first.' Light as a butterfly, Runty tiptoed along a water pipe that led to a ledge. From there, the air-con a floor below was only a jump away. *Leap!*

Stolly's sad little face peered from the air-con above. 'Did it hurt?'

Runty looked down. The ground was only one floor away and the pipe layout was the same. He crawled along the water pipe, reached the ledge, and leapt. The ground felt soft and wet under his paws.

'What about me?' called Stolly.

'What about you?'

Stolly stayed stuck in a fug of fear. 'I daren't,' he whimpered.

'Serves you right for eating my tuna.' Runty sniffed. Never mind losing a few mouthfuls of fish. What interesting new smells there were outside.

Stolly reached out to test the pipe with a paw. *Holy cats!* It wobbled a bit. He sank into it and, taking a deep breath, crawled along it in a snaky kind of way.

One shuffle. Two shuffles. Three shuffles, four. He reached the ledge. And the big dog yawn suddenly didn't seem so scary. *Leap!*

He landed heavily on the air-con below.

'Not bad for a fattie,' meowed Runty, turning away to sniff a flower.

One shuffle, two shuffles, three shuffles – *uh oh!* – Stolly's outer paws slipped off the pipe and he almost fell.

On the last air-con, his legs seized up again.

'Close your eyes and jump,' called Runty.

Crash! Stolly landed. His legs hurt. And for a horrible moment, he thought Runty had disappeared.

Until his nose poked out of a nearby bush. 'I thought you'd never make it.'

'That's it. I've had enough of your teasing. I'm off. Goodbye!' Stolly turned tail, stopped.

He looked up. Dark trees towered above him like giants.

'Well I'm waiting here,' meowed Runty.

'For what?'

Runty licked a muddy paw. 'Morning.'

'And then?'

'June will find us and carry us home.'

'What about Mama?'

'What about her?'

'Don't you want to see her again?'

'Not tonight,' said Runty.

'Well, *I'm* going to find her!' meowed Stolly, and scampered across the grass.

'Come back,' called Runty.

Chapter 7
Everyone Has a Papa Somewhere

Stolly kept running. Up the hill, along a track. His legs felt shaky and the air ruffled his fur in a scary way but he kept running. 'Mama? Mama?' he called.

What about Mama June? Runty thought crossly. She'd feel so sad not to find him on her bed when she woke up. And she'd serve salmon biscuits for breakfast. He groaned at the memory of Mama Mao's lizards and rats.

'I think I hear cats!' called Stolly disappearing behind a corner.

Rats, thought Runty. He bounded up the hill, twitching his ears for anything that may jump out from between the trees. An owl hooted, as if to criticize him for being mean to his big brother.

He soon caught up with Stolly, who stopped abruptly at the top of the hill, nearly knocking Runty over.

Below, in a moonlit clearing, hundreds of caterwauling cats circled a boulder. A fat tom cat sat high on top of it, protected by two guards. Was it the Discovery Bay cat clan? The one which Mama belonged to?

'Can you see her?' Stolly meowed breathlessly. The kittens moved closer and hid behind a tree trunk.

But it was impossible to spot Mama among the heaving bodies.

The tom cat howled to the crescent moon. Scars criss-crossed his chest. He must have had many fights. 'Hey, he's a tabby, like me,' meowed Runty.

'But where's Mama?' meowed Stolly.

'Shut up, everyone,' yowled one of the guards. The one with a missing tail.

'Big Boss wants to start the meeting,' yowled the one who was missing an ear.

Then there was only the droning of night insects. Something scurried behind the kittens and Runty clenched his claws.

Big Boss stood on all four paws and cleared his throat. 'With deep regret, I have to report the disappearance of more cats,' he began, 'Kit Cat, Mogs, Pussy Willow ... as well as my dear wife, Mama Mao.'

There were howls of shock and anger.

The loudest and longest was Stolly's. *Mama Mao?* His mama? She'd disappeared? Well, he knew that. But Big Boss made her disappearance sound so ... so final. Stolly's fur rippled as a chill passed through his body.

Mama Mao. My dear wife? Before Runty could think, Big Boss and the guards were staring in his direction.

Then hundreds of cats' eyes were staring too.

'Come on out, whoever you are,' called Big Boss.

'Spies!' howled a cat.

'They're spies from another clan!' yowled another.

'Catch, catch, catch, catch!' howled all the clan members.

Stolly felt blood drain from his face as the guards raced towards them.

Runty puffed up, his fur spiked as a porcupine. Scraggy Ear snarled, looming over him. 'What's your business?'

'N-othing,' Runty stammered.

'What about ugly Half Tail here?' growled the one with no tail at all.

Stolly froze. He could hardly breathe, never mind speak.

Runty shuddered. The guard bullying Stolly was also missing an eye. Was he blind? 'Say something, Stolly,' he meowed.

'Shut up,' snarled One Eye.

Ow! Even if One Eye couldn't see properly, he could certainly bite. Runty shook himself off the iron teeth that pinched his neck.

'You're both cat food, mate,' said Scraggy Ear, pushing Stolly down the path.

A strong stink of bird grew stronger. The wild cats hissed and clawed the kittens as they were cat-marched to Big Boss, who jumped off his rock and banged his tail.

He narrowed his eyes and stared, coming

close, far too close. 'Explain yourself,' he growled.

'We were looking ... f-f-for our mother,' stammered Runty.

Big Boss bared his needle-sharp teeth. 'You think I believe that?'

'Why not?' meowed Runty.

Scraggy Ear swiped Runty's chest. 'Don't be cheeky!'

Then something clicked in Runty's brain. 'I should tell you that Mama Mao is our mama, so I think *you* must be our papa.'

Big Boss swivelled his long neck and growled.

'He's our papa? I don't understand,' whispered Stolly.

'Shhh,' said Runty. How could his big brother be so dumb?

'Give 'em the sniff test, Boss,' meowed One Eye.

Big Boss seemed to think that was a good

idea. He unclenched his claws and sniffed Runty.

He sniffed again. His whiskers tickled.

He sniffed Stolly, who trembled like a trapped toad.

He turned tail and said, 'Follow me into my lair.'

'Meeting postponed,' yowled Scraggy Ear and One Eye, butting the kittens along.

He's going to kill us, thought Runty miserably, recalling how many other tabbies there had been in the crowd. Big Boss probably had hundreds of kitty babies. Why should he care about *them*?

The lair was strewn with lizard tails, bird claws and frog skin. One Eye offered the kittens one palm leaf mat each to sit on.

Papa Mao sat on the biggest palm leaf and fluffed out his chest. 'I am now satisfied that you *are* my fluff and fur,' he meowed.

Runty sighed with relief but Stolly still

shook. Runty nudged him when Big Boss turned his back toward a cat skull hanging on the wall.

Papa Mao's eyes flashed angrily. 'And as my fluff and fur, I don't doubt your courage, unlike some of my other sons,' he growled.

Cats disappearing nightly, traps, nets, poisoned rats. Runty's little brain fizzed when Big Boss told them what had been happening. All Big Boss's sons had either gone missing themselves, or had run away. A scout called Old Fuzzy Paws had recently reported seeing cats being driven away in a white-coloured van.

'Is it driven by a white-haired woman?' Runty meowed.

'Don't interrupt,' snarled Scraggy Ear.

Big Boss twitched his whiskers. He had the longest whiskers Stolly had ever seen.

Runty clenched his claws.

But Big Boss lay down and ordered some rainwater. 'We've sent the information along the meow network to the Lion Rock King,' he said wearily, 'but for some reason haven't heard anything back.'

Now Mama Mao had once told the kittens about Hong Kong's cat communication network. If any members of the cat family – cats, lions, tigers – needed to communicate something important, they would tell each other by passing a message along the meow network. The Lion Rock King lived at the heart of it on the top of a famous mountain in a place called Kowloon.

As if excited by something, Papa Mao pushed the banana husk of water aside and stood up. His eyes flamed. 'You *are* both extraordinarily brave, like me, right?'

Runty's heart beat fast but he meowed yes.

Stolly tried to open his mouth but couldn't.

Papa Mao glared at him. 'Did you say something?'

'Ye-ees.' His voice sounded as squeaky as a mouse.

Papa Mao narrowed his eyes. 'I command

you to travel to Kowloon to see the Lion Rock King. Report that cats are missing and then follow his orders.'

Chapter 8

A Dancing Lion

When the sky turned pink and the birds began to sing, Papa Mao led his sons down to the ferry pier. 'Catch a boat,' he meowed. 'When you reach land, ask a member of the cat family to show you the way to the Lion Rock King. But I should warn you, human land is full of danger.'

Sure enough, in the plaza, bony men wheeled overloaded trolleys to supermarkets. Lively dogs pulled owners for walks. School children kicked balls.

A ferry horn hooted and some humans rushed past. Papa Mao nosed the kittens goodbye and snuck away.

'What now?' meowed Stolly nervously.

Runty glanced around. The area between them and the pier was paved in concrete and there wasn't a tree in sight. *Why did Stolly always ask* him *what to do?* He trotted to the nearest bush and hid underneath it.

Stolly followed suit.

Watching humans move to and fro became a bit boring, until a grandma parked a pram and went inside a nearby shop. She was dressed smartly and carrying some empty shopping bags. Runty would bet his bottom whisker that she was going into town. 'After me!' he meowed.

While the grandma was in the shop, the kittens jumped into the pram and took cover under the baby's blanket. It felt warm. Too warm. And it was hard to breathe. What the baby couldn't say in words, she did with her legs. *Kick, kick!*

Next minute, the kittens felt themselves pushed across the concrete and bumping down a ramp.

'Ouch,' meowed Stolly.

Driing! A bell rang. The ferry was about to depart. At last, it seemed they were on their way. Runty gave Stolly's ear a comforting lick.

'I feel sick,' meowed Stolly.

'Sssh,' said Runty.

Luckily for the kittens, the grandma was deaf.

The boat rocked and rolled in the water and there was the smell of salt and water. Then the rocking and rolling stilled and the ferry docked at Central.

From the waterfront came the beating of drums and the clang of gongs. What was going on? Runty could barely hear himself think. He peeked out.

It was a colourful parade, a moving procession of humans and banners and bobbing balloons. At the head, a lively Chinese lion with a squirmy snake body and a shaggy white mane.

The baby started to cry.

'Goodness me,' cried Grandma as the kittens jumped out of the pram and disappeared into the crowd.

The dancing lion blinked his eyes and flapped its ears when he saw the kittens. 'Good morning,' he said. 'Not often you see kitties in these parts.'

'We're looking for the Lion Rock K—'

Runty's voice was drowned by the banging drums and crashing cymbals and the lion danced away.

'Wait!' meowed Runty.

'You're looking for the Lion Rock King, you

say?' called the lion, above the racket. It jerked his head towards the high-rise buildings ahead. 'Go to Mr. and Mrs. HSBC. They should be able to help you.'

Mr. and Mrs. HSBC? What a strange name. Why HSBC?

'Hey, a pussy cat!' shouted a boy, pulling away from his mother and running towards Stolly.

'Help!' Stolly turned tail and bolted down the promenade.

'Wait!' called Runty.

Chapter 9
Who's Boss Now?

Buses spouted smelly fumes. Trams clanked on rickety tracks. One stopped suddenly and its angry driver shook a fist at a Shanghai dumpling delivery man.

'There they are!' meowed Runty. On the other side of the busy street, on a black plinth, beside a long-legged Lego-like building, crouched two giant lions. They looked stony-faced but there was a sparkle in their eyes, as if they could come alive at any minute.

The kittens ran across the black and white zebra stripes, taking care to avoid human feet.

As they approached the magnificent lions, they lifted their tails high with respect.

'Yes, I'm Mr. HSBC and she's my missus,' said the lion around the ball between his jagged teeth.

'Made in Britain with the finest bronze,' boasted Mrs. HSBC.

'And *this* is the heart of Hong Kong,' said Mr. HSBC, waving a paw at the skyscraper forest that surrounded them.

At that moment, there was an angry roar.

The kittens raised their hackles and scanned the land. In the distance, Runty spotted two other lion statues sitting outside the Bank of China. Their mane hair was curled tight and their greedy eyes glittered in the afternoon sun.

'Ignore Mr. and Mrs. HSBC,' roared Mr. BOC. 'Come and talk to us. We own this territory now.'

'And the future is mine,' squeaked a lion cub, pinioned under Mrs. BOC's claws.

Mr. HSBC rolled his eyes.

With a fast-beating heart, Runty started to tell him about Mama Mao and the missing cats of the Discovery Bay cat clan ... until a passing school girl dangled something delicious in front of Stolly. 'You like beef jerky?'

Stolly licked his lips.

'Keep away,' meowed Runty.

But Stolly extended his neck and twitched his nose.

Holy cats! The girl leaned down to stroke

him. Stolly spat and hissed. The school girl dropped the beef jerky and ran.

But another human had stopped by too. 'Don't be afraid, kitty cats,' he said.

Stolly bolted, Runty too, and the man raced around trying to catch them.

'Jump into my belly,' urged Mrs. HSBC.

'Don't do it,' snapped Mrs. BOC, with sharp teeth.

'It's a trick,' roared Mr. BOC.

'Nonsense,' hollered Mr. HSBC. 'These cats have important business for the Lion Rock King.'

But now the pavement was crowded with humans trying to snare the kittens.

Quick as lightning, they leapt up and slid into Mrs. HSBC's mouth.

It was dark inside but there was some cooling rainwater to drink.

Chapter 10
To Nine Dragon Mountains, M'goy

Stolly woke up early next morning with a tummy aching for food. So when a sparrow landed on the head of Mrs. HSBC, Mr. HSBC lifted a paw and knocked it dead.

The city was already awake. Cars honked. Brakes screeched. A group of school children were trying to break into Mrs. HSBC's rusty belly. *Time to move on,* thought Runty.

'Travel in the direction of the Nine Dragons,' said Mrs. HSBC, pointing to a distant mountain range. 'And if you get lost, ask for Lion Rock.'

'Thank you for your hospitality,' meowed the kittens, the taste of fresh bird on their lips.

The kittens jumped on the first bus that came along. 'Cats!' shrieked an old lady. She swung her shopping bag at them as they ran upstairs.

Hiding under a seat, Stolly buried his head under Runty hoping nobody else would notice them.

But they were on their way. The bus stopped and started. Legs came and went. Mobile telephones rang and beeped. Gradually, the bus gained speed and there were fewer stops.

After what seemed like forever, the chattering ceased and the engine stalled.

Silence. Runty peeked out from under the seat. No humans anymore. No more shops and offices. Just butterflies and flowers, mountains and sky.

The driver put his feet on the steering wheel and slurped some tea.

Runty tiptoed out from under the seat,

jumped onto it, stood on his hind legs and looked out the window.

There, towering above, were the opening arms of a beautiful mountain. Mops of green tree heads morphed into a green meadow. Stolly would be able to catch lots of butterflies there.

Runty looked higher, to the place where pillow white clouds pierced the summit. There, solid grey rock became a craggy head. An arching back. Two stone paws. Runty's heart beat strongly against his ribs. 'That's the Lion Rock King,' he meowed, 'I'm sure of it.'

'Can you see Mama?' meowed Stolly.

'Shhh!' Runty had forgotten all about the driver. He dived down to the floor and sneaked to the back of the bus. Thank his lucky star! One of the passenger windows was open.

He slipped through it easily, landing safely.

Stolly, still stuffed full of bird, tried to follow. Head, front legs – no problem. But his tummy? No way. He pushed and pulled. He even tried going backwards.

Worried that his brother would get completely stuck, that the driver would drive off with him inside, Runty ran round the bus to see if there was any other way out.

What was that thunderous noise?

The driver. Snoring. He'd left the front entrance open.

Runty bounded up the stairs. 'This way. Fast as you can,' he meowed.

Stolly ran down the corridor, pussyfooted past the snoring man, jumped off the bus ... and landed in a puddle, spraying Runty with mud.

'You idiocat!' Runty licked off the dirty drops from his coat.

Offended, Stolly dipped his tongue in the puddle. 'I'm so thirsty.'

'I am too. But if you drink that, you'll puke!'

Mmm, the water did taste a little bit like June's socks. Stolly wiped his tongue on a palm leaf.

Runty wrinkled his nose sniffing the fresh air. 'Ready?'

With green grass under happy paw, the kittens ran up the mountain path. Stolly recalled Mama Mao's sweet smile and nearly overtook his brother.

But it was Runty who heard the water first. He padded down to the bank of a gurgling creek. Careful not to wet his paws, he drank deeply. What a pleasure it was to feel cool water sliding down his throat.

Stolly drank faster. At least he could beat his runt of a brother at something.

Not far away, tucked behind a rock, hid a large Burmese python. The kind of snake who liked to eat red meat. The kind that could, quick as a blink, grab hold of kitties and suffocate them.

Boo the Burmese python slithered nearer. His tongue flicked in and out of his scaly mouth, slicing the air.

"Kittens," he hissed. "Kittens for dinner."

Chapter 11
Twit Twoo I Do

Ten feet long, car-tyre thick, Boo the Burmese python could squeeze little kittens into bags of bones. Sliding closer, he lowered his head.

Snake, snake! cautioned the birds on a papaya tree.

Runty pricked his ears. *What a noisy bunch of feathers,* he thought.

Boo coiled his body, ready to attack, when ... what was that?

The *yip yip* of a wild dog.

The kittens didn't need dog language to understand the warning. Runty zipped up the nearest tree. Stolly scampered up the bank and ran along the path.

Hissing with anger, Boo snaked after him.

Stolly ran, faster, faster than he'd ever run before. His hot paws pounded. Dust filled his nostrils. How could that legless snake move so fast? For a few scary seconds, Boo seemed to be catching up.

'Climb a tree!' howled Runty.

But Stolly, in a panic, kept running along the path. It was climbing and he could barely catch his breath. Higher and higher. Steeper and steeper. He ran until he couldn't run any more.

Thank his lucky star! Ahead, the slippery slope of a landslide. At its base, a patchwork of dead trees. Stolly leapt down – down, down – and landed on a nest of branches. It was far, far too far for Boo to reach.

The python gave an angry hiss and snaked back through the bushes to sulk in his hole by the river bank. He would wait. When the kitten returned to his brother, he would attack again.

Stolly lay shivering until the sun went down. His nose felt dry as a plum. His mouth flinty as granite. A lonely feeling hung heavy in his belly and just wouldn't go away. 'Mama, Mama,' he meowed.

There was no reply.

'Runty, Runty,' he howled, then worried that the snake would hear him.

At last, darkness fell. The cooler air calmed him. It was now or never. Stolly twitched his tail and straightened his whiskers. At least with his night vision, he could see clearly.

But where could his brother be? Stolly walked and walked. He sniffed the stones. He listened for clues.

All he could hear was the buzzing of mosquitoes. And the cries of strange night creatures.

'Have you seen my brother?' he asked a bat.

The bat flitted down and brushed against his ear. 'Does he have a funny tail, like you?'

How rude!

Stolly called to the fireflies who were flickering around him. 'Have you seen my brother?'

But they just twinkled like lost stars.

Stolly yowled.

'You're hurting my ears,' hooted Sara the owl.

Stolly followed her hoot. Wings outstretched, she was about to alight from a mango tree. 'Oh

please, don't fly away. You don't know where my brother is, do you?' he meowed.

Stolly felt her yellow eyes boring into his. Sara liked to help lost animals. She'd helped many a lost soul in her time.

'*Twit twoo,* I do. Follow me,' she said.

Never had the kittens felt so happy to see each other again.

Runty licked Stolly's face and neck.

Stolly licked Runty's face, neck, shoulders and muddy paws. Even his smelly butt. Exhausted, he lay his head on Runty's belly.

Runty wrapped his tail around him. 'Did you feel scared?'

Stolly twitched his whiskers. 'Not really.'

Runty tapped them with his tail. 'I don't believe you.'

Stolly raised his heavy head. 'Well, a little bit.'

'Why didn't you climb the tree, like I told you?'

Runty paused. 'Because I'm fed up of being told what to do? By you, my *little* brother.'

Runty gave Stolly's neck a playful nip.

'Good night, sweet dreams, kitties,' screeched Sara, flapping off towards a watery moon.

Chapter 12
The Lion Rock King

At last, the kittens reached the top of the mountain. Under the late afternoon sun, the Lion Rock King's head shone like a magical place. Far down below, city skyscrapers blinked. Cruise ships winked.

Hungry and thirsty, the kittens clawed their way up Lion Rock King's bony backbone. They scaled a lumpy rock.

'Who's tickling my ear?' murmured the Lion Rock King. Stones bounced down the valley.

Holy cats! The kittens felt stones shifting

under their paws. They flexed their claws as they struggled to stay put.

'Who's that *scratching* my ear?' said the Lion Rock King.

The bouncing stones became an avalanche and a warm rush of air nearly blew the kittens to the last of their lives. The Lion Rock King was yawning!

'Help! Help!' cried Stolly, hanging on to the

king's lip by the skin of his paws.

With a flick of his tongue, the Lion Rock King flipped the trembling kittens onto his upturned paw. 'Who are you, small fry?'

Runty gulped. 'I'm ... we're ... the sons of Big Boss, your majesty.'

'And we've lost our mother,' squeaked Stolly.

As the Lion Rock King listened to their story, his body turned golden in the evening sun. 'Don't worry, you two. I must have overslept. These long sunny summer days are so pleasant up here.'

'So pleasant,' repeated Stolly, as if in a trance.

Runty sunk a little lower into the king's comfortable pad. Maybe everything would be alright after all.

'I believe the cats have been kidnapped,' said the Lion Rock King 'Kidnapping – and catnapping for that matter – is a serious crime. So there's no time to waste. I'll make an announcement. Shelter behind that boulder.

When the Lion Rock lowered them to the ground, Stolly and Runty ran towards where he'd pointed to.

The Lion Rock King inhaled deeply, his belly swelled, and he let out a deafening roar.

One royal roar and all members of the meow network froze to hear his royal decree:

'Attention all members of the cat family. Mama Mao has gone missing. Many other cats too. I order everyone to seek them without delay.'

Wild cats passed the message to stone lions guarding village houses in Shatin. Village house stone lions passed the message to stone lions guarding banks. Stuffed lions in toy shops heard it and passed it to lions in Shenzhen zoo. Chinese air was alive with cat messaging.

Runty's ears swung like radar.

Stolly's heart beat as fast as butterfly wings.

Kites circled above. Crows cawed. But there was no howling. No yowling. Not even the scuffling of mice.

Runty looked for signs of movement, but there wasn't any.

Stolly's tail drooped. Maybe his worst nightmare was true. Mama Mao really was dead.

The Lion Rock King shrugged his flanks. The sun had slipped away and the moon shone brighter. 'I'll make another announcement tomorrow,' he said.

Runty bowed low. 'At your majesty's pleasure.'

'But why not now?' Stolly blurted. He scratched the ground as if he wanted to bury himself.

'Don't be so rude,' meowed Runty, head-butting him.

Lion Rock King twitched his whiskers, and looked east. 'Come back at sunrise. Go down the mountain now. Find some shelter. I'd prefer to be alone.'

'Yes, your majesty.' Runty bowed again.

'What? We're leaving already?' meowed Stolly.

Runty pushed his brother down the path.

Stolly looked back. The Lion Rock King's eyes were already closed. With a heavy heart, he turned tail and ordered his stiff legs to keep moving. 'We're never going to find mama, alive or dead,' he meowed.

But far away, there was a faint roar, followed by another, louder now. Then there was the howling and yowling of cats, lots and lots of cats. Was it news about Mama?

The kittens scampered back up to the mountain top.

A black cat was about to report to the Lion Rock King. She cleared her throat and puffed up her chest. 'We hear of unusual human activity in the no-man's land between Hong Kong and China.'

The Lion Rock King nodded thoughtfully.

Unusual activity – what did that mean? Stolly grit his teeth with frustration when the cat puffed up her chest some more. Why had she stopped talking?

Runty was all ears too. *No-man's land*? Was that a land where there were no humans?

'Continue,' said the Lion Rock King.

The wild cat purred. 'There's a new restaurant there. It sells cat soup. Hundreds of cats are locked up in cages there. On death row.'

Chapter 13
Sometimes Dogs are Cats' Best Friends

Night fell. The moon shone brighter than lampposts, softening the tufts of mountain grass. Hungry and thirsty, the kittens ran in the direction the wild cat had pointed to. She was too tired to go with them.

Runty, head held high, led the way. For some reason, he kept thinking of June. He hoped she wasn't missing him too much.

Meanwhile, Stolly dreamed of cuddling up to Mama Mao and licking her kind face.

They could tell from a terrible smell that

they'd nearly reached the restaurant. A high wall, as high as the sky, loomed over them.

A big shaggy dog came bounding round the corner. 'Good evening, I thought you'd never arrive,' she barked.

Runty hissed.

'Don't be afraid of *me*,' woofed the dog. 'I'm Milly and I've been sent by the restaurant's guard dogs.'

Was Milly tricking them? Her eyes looked friendly. Her nose quivered. She was even wagging her tail.

'Proof,' said Runty. 'I want proof.'

Milly led them to a hole in the wall, from where the kittens espied a shabby building. Cars slept under an aluminium roof.

'That,' said Milly, 'is a cat soup restaurant.'

Two big dogs strained against their chains.

'We're over here,' Milly called, 'Me and the Discovery Bay cat clan kittens.'

The heavy chains clinked against the concrete as the guard dogs stopped straining and sat on their haunches.

Milly gently nosed Runty forwards.

She tried to introduce Stolly too but he spiked his fur and hissed.

'Well met, Milly,' barked one of the dogs. 'We could smell that they were nearby.'

Runty brushed his fur against Milly's hairy legs to show his thanks.

Above the dimly lit building was a neon sign. Runty couldn't read the words but a snarling cat picture told him all he needed to know.

Stolly had noticed it too. He un-puffed his fur but still felt shaky inside. 'Do you think Mama is in there?' he meowed.

'Almost certainly,' said Milly, 'unless, you know, she's been—'

'Saved by us.' Runty extended his claws and pretended to swipe at a bird.

At that moment, a rat scuttled towards them. 'Hurry up!' it squeaked.

There was the splutter of an old engine and the flash of headlights. It was that dirty old white van again. 'I'd better get back to duty,' Milly said, disappearing through the hole.

'Follow me!' said the rat.

That's a first, thought Runty. A cat, following a rat.

Hidden in the shadows, Milly observed the newly arrived humans. The old woman had brought a child with her. She listened to their conversation as they walked towards the restaurant and wished she could understand.

'So this is Cat Soup Shack?'

'What do you think it is?'

'You drive here, once a week, with all your captured cats?'

Old Aunt Po winced. 'Only *cats*. I never bring kittens.'

Meanwhile, the rat had led the kittens to the back of the restaurant.

'Pooh!' said Stolly.

Smoke poured out of a dirty funnel. A putrid smell of cheap cooking oil and rotting meat filled the air. But one window was slightly ajar.

With a swish of his tail, a bunching of his hind legs, Runty sprung up to the sill.

The moment Runty landed, a chorus of cats meowed, 'Help! Help!'

What a shocking sight! There were hundreds of cats, locked inside cages, clawing and meowing. The cages were piled as high as the kitchen ceiling.

'What can you see up there?' Stolly called.

Runty hardly dare tell him. He saw flames, heard the roar of gas. A cook was sizzling meat in a wok. A carver, wearing a blood-stained apron, was pouring steaming water into a pot.

'Can you see Mama?'

Runty scanned the cages. There were so many of them.

Impatient, Stolly tried to leap as high as the window sill, but failed.

'Have you lost your voice?'

Runty's tail slipped out of sight.

'Runty,' howled Stolly. He leapt as high as he could, hit the wall, and fell to the ground, yowling.

Milly bounded towards him. 'Are you hurt?'

'Just my silly little tail,' said Stolly miserably.

'You can do it, Stolly,' she said. 'Try again.'

Stolly backed up. He ran towards the window sill, faster and faster ... and performed the jump of his life.

To his surprise, his front legs landed on the window sill. He'd made it, just!

Stolly's ears rang with cat howls. 'Meow, meow, MIAOW,' the captured cats cried.

'Runty?' cried Stolly.

'Here,' Runty meowed. He'd jumped on top of a kitchen cupboard. 'Look! Over there!'

Stolly faced the maze of cages in a daze. But then he heard the voice, saw the face, he'd been longing for.

'Mama, Mama!' he cried.

'Stolly!' cried Mama Mao. Her nose was pressed against her cage, and her body squashed in the middle of a heaving mass of cats.

Chapter 14
Cat Soup

The door between the restaurant and the kitchen swung open and a rush of fried fish and barbecued meat greeted the kittens' noses. Inside, the kittens saw dishes piled high on tables. Hungry humans chopsticking away at them. 'Cat soup for table four, Cissy,' shouted a waiter.

'Two more cats, Carver Jo,' shouted the Cissy the cook, turning up the gas. She'd need to make another batch of soup to keep up with demand.

The kittens didn't understand her words.

But the smell in the smoky air told them everything.

Carver Jo's eyes roved over the cages of shivering animals. He unhooked a door and lifted up a black and white cat by the scruff of her neck.

'Stop!' yowled Runty. It felt as if the hand was grabbing his own body. He jumped down to where Stolly was, aligned his body to attack.

But then the door flapped open again and someone was shouting their names. The voice sounded familiar.

It was June. 'Runty!' she shouted.

Old Aunt Po limped behind her.

'There's Stolly too,' June cried, rushing to the window. 'I told you it was them.'

The kittens were so surprised, they froze.

June grabbed Runty and held him in her arms. He struggled but she held him tight. Tears dripped down her face.

Stolly howled. What was June doing here? Why had she caught Runty? Was she going to take him back to her home? She seemed very happy to see them again.

'I told you, I don't catch *kittens,*' grumbled Old Aunt Po.

Stolly yowled. How else could he show June that he'd found his darling mama? That she was in grave danger? That he'd never lose her again?

June tried to kiss Runty. Seizing the moment, Runty wriggled out of her grip and jumped back up to the kitchen cupboard.

YOWL! What he saw from up there gave him tiger strength. Carver Jo was rooting in Mama Mao's cage.

He poked a cat, then another, checking for the meatiest one.

Stolly, suddenly realising what was happening, yowled too.

Mama Mao! Carver Jo had picked her!

Chapter 15
The Rescue

Now cats are not stupid. Like pigs and cows, they know when they're about to die. Snake meat and chicken were sizzling in Cissy's wok. She'd stirred in the tree fungus, black mushrooms and fish glue. She'd sprinkled the ginger, scallion and spices.

Now all her cat soup needed was two cats.

Mama Mao dangled from Carver Jo's hands.

'Attack!' yowled Runty, flying from the cupboard. He landed on Carver Jo and sank his claws into his shoulder.

'*Ow!*' shrieked Carver Jo.

'Anything wrong?' shouted Cissy from above the roar of her wok.

Meanwhile, Stolly was ripping at Carver Jo's leg. The carver dropped Mama Mao, who landed awkwardly on her hind legs.

Cissy waved her cooking spoon wildly at the kittens. 'Get off him!' she shouted.

Round and round the kitchen the cats ran, with Cissy and her cooking spoon closely behind. *Swipe!* She missed Runty by a whisker.

Runty leapt out of the window, Mama Mao close behind.

Swipe! Cissy smacked Stolly's butt. Her swipe propelled him to the window.

The Mao family raced to the wall and hid under a bush.

'Mama!' cried Stolly, burying his nose in Mama Mao's fur. She was thinner than ever, much less furry. But she smelt sweet as milk.

'My leg hurts,' meowed Mama Mao. It looked broken.

'What happened?' meowed Stolly, trying to nose it better.

Runty paused for breath. They were safe. They were together. Now they should all run away from this death trap immediately. But ... he hesitated. June had discovered where they were hiding. She was lying under the bush shining a blinding torch in his eyes. She seemed determined to catch them.

And there was Old Aunt Po standing behind her, looking very old and sad.

Runty remembered June's tears of joy when she found them. Did he really want to run away from her?

June inch-wormed towards him. 'There are three of them!' she said, lunging at Runty.

Runty side-stepped away.

'And one of them, the adult, is bleeding.' June shuffled on her knees, vainly trying to reach Mama Mao. 'Oh please, please come out of there,' she said.

Mama Mao was too weak to move.

Stolly sprang forward and blocked June with snarls and hisses. He pounced at her and sunk his teeth into her arm.

'Ow!' cried June.

That decided Runty. June didn't deserve that. They should let themselves be caught. Let her take them back to her home. All of them. They'd be safe there. 'Your leg needs time to mend,' he pleaded with Mama Mao. 'You'll never have to hunt again.'

Mama Mao tried to move her leg. It really did hurt.

Stolly's tail hurt badly too. Suddenly the

thought of running back into that black night of wild dogs and cheeky bats frightened him. And, even if they did run back, what if Mama Mao couldn't run fast enough? Or she ran off somewhere else and was bitten by that angry snake?

Maybe Runty was right.

Mama Mao, sensing Stolly's indecision, feeling the searing pain in her leg, rubbed her cheek against Stolly's. She felt so relieved to be re-united with her darling sons.

'Wait 'til you taste June's tuna,' Stolly meowed bravely.

Tuna? Mama Mao hadn't eaten fish before.

Maybe she'd stay with them. For a moon, or two.

'Thank you for saving me, my boys,' she meowed.

Twinkle Toes

Chapter 1
The Best Birthday Present Ever

Every Saturday morning, grandma Pau Pau leaves me on a bus in Tung Chung, and Dad picks me up in Mui Wo.

Every Saturday morning, Dad scoops me off the bus, and kisses me once on the cheek.

Today was special. Grown-ups stood at the bus shelter looking and pointing. What was happening?

Dad was wearing sunglasses. 'Happy Birthday, Twinkle Toes,' he said, kissing me three times. I passed him my crutches and instead of lowering me to the ground, he raised me high.

And that's when I saw her!

A pony! A real pony! Dappled grey with a white striped head. Long grey legs. Her tail swished like a rattan broom.

'She's yours,' Dad said.

I laughed aloud. I couldn't believe it. Such a big animal.

As Dad carried me to my pony the people in the bus shelter *ooh*-ed and *ah*-ed. 'It's the Year of the Horse after all,' he said.

She smelt of grass. Her muzzle felt like silk.

She had deep brown eyes and the longest eyelashes I'd ever seen.

'Does she bite?'

Dad ruffled my hair. 'Of course not.'

Heave! He lifted me onto her back.

Ouch! Her backbone dug into my you-know-what.

'Let's be going then,' said Dad, untying the reins from the lamppost.

'Wait!' I cried. The ground seemed a long way down.

'Grip with those thighs of yours,' said Dad, jerking my pony's mouth. With a lurch, she stepped off the pavement. I had to grab her shaggy mane to keep from sliding off.

Clip clop. Clip clop. Down the village path we walked. Me, swinging to the rhythm of my pony's giant steps. Dad, crutches in hand, whistling a jolly tune. 'A pony for the Year of the Horse,' I said.

Cyclists slowed down. Hikers stopped and pointed. Wild dogs ran for cover.

Chapter 2
Sold for a Song

I woke up the next day thinking, *Wow, maybe I'm the only kid in Hong Kong who has a pony!*

Dad said she was flown in from Mongolia to carry heavy rods for the new cable car to the Big Buddha. Then, when the project was finished, she was sold for a song.

'Sold for a song?'

Dad grinned. 'She didn't break my bank, anyway.'

Dad says the oddest things sometimes. That's because he's English, not Chinese like Ma and grandma Pau Pau.

We tried out a few names but chose *Sukee* because my pony nodded her head when I whispered it down her ear.

I made up my own song while Dad led us to the waterfall:

Sukee, Sukee super star,
What a lovely pet you are.

Dad told me ponies eat stacks of grass but that's one thing he has. His house is a bit of a dump but there's a field nearby. A big green one.

'Only grass?' I said.

'And lots of TLC, like me,' said Dad.

I giggled.

Tender loving care. I give Dad lots even though Pau Pau and Ma say unkind things about him. He says he gives me lots because he loves me to bits.

To keep ponies, you also need:

- a halter (to tie your pony to a post);
- a bridle (so you can steer and stop);

- a saddle (Dad said he's saving); and,
- a grooming kit (to clean your pony).

Dad tethered Sukee to a tree. The waterfall frothed like lemonade. As I threw pebbles, Dad climbed up the rocks and sat on one mushroom smooth. 'I name this *Sukee stone*,' he said.

When my foot is better, I'm going to climb up there too and carve Sukee's name on it.

We ate peanut-butter sandwiches until mosquitoes starting eating us.

Nearly home, Ronny's dog – BC – bounded up to say hello and Sukee flicked her ears back and snorted. Ronny – Dad's next-door neighbour who built the new airport with Dad – waved from his vegetable patch.

Dad filled a bucket with water. 'How about we take Sukee down to the beach tomorrow?' he said. 'Ponies can swim, you know.'

Wa! How did she learn that? Amazed, I offered her a handful of grass. Her lips tickled my hand and made me laugh.

After a dinner of baked beans on toast, I called home. Pau Pau answered and told me Ma was on a late shift. I was about to tell her about Sukee when Dad did his hand-across-the-neck slice. Strange he knows what I'm saying even though he doesn't speak Cantonese.

S'pose I understand his sign language: that slice means *don't tell.*

So I let Pau Pau blab on about the price of pork instead.

Chapter 3
Sukee and I Go Swimming

The sun was shining egg-yolk yellow. I sang:

Sukee, Sukee super star,
You're all mine and we'll go far, far.

'To the beach?' said Dad.

Yeah! To Silvermine Bay! 'But isn't the water too dirty?'

'Try the Med,' said Dad.

We tried to catch Sukee. Pacing the field, Dad clicked his tongue, called her name, rattled the pony nuts. But Sukee didn't bother to raise

her head. I bit the end of a pony nut. *Yuk!* It tasted like Dad's favourite Stilton cheese. No wonder Sukee wasn't interested.

Dad approached Sukee slowly, hoping she'd put her nose in the bucket so he could slip the halter around her neck.

Ha ha! As soon as he got within snatch distance she turned tail and trotted away.

At last, Dad caught her, and I was riding down to the beach on her back, smelling the delicious sizzle of people barbecuing chicken wings.

'What a beauty!' called Mrs. Potts, being pulled along by a lively dog. She is a physiotherapist who rescues abandoned pets.

Sukee's ears pricked and she whinnied softly when she saw the sparkling sea. On the beach, her knees buckled: she wanted to roll in the sand!

Dad shouted at her to stop.

Yikes! I could have got squashed.

Dad stripped down to his swimming trunks and led us to the shore.

'Shouldn't I be wearing a rubber ring?'

Dad pressed against my good leg. 'Don't worry, Twinks. You're in good hands.'

Sukee didn't seem at all afraid of the water, wading deeper and deeper, snorting and splashing. I wrapped my arms around her long neck. Dad floated on his back. Then we were riding the waves together. I was a mermaid. Dad a merman. Sukee a merpony.

Some people gathered on the shore to watch us. A Chinese boy called, 'Can I have a ride?' He was with a grown-up carrying a birdcage.

'What's he saying?' asked Dad.

I translated.

'Yes, for ten dollars,' said Dad.

Ha ha! Maybe we could get rich by charging money for pony rides.

Maybe not. The boy frowned.

Then Dad winked at me.

I pulled on Sukee's reins and urged her towards the shore.

Chapter 4
Money Bird

'Will Sukee catch cold?' I asked, running my hand along her coat to squeeze the water out.

Dad laughed. '*You* will, if you don't dry yourself.'

The boy followed us up the beach to my towel. He was stringy as runner bean and had thick black hair. He cautiously reached for Sukee's neck and patted her. 'Is she yours?' he asked.

I nodded proudly.

'Tan Tan, your shoes are wet,' grumbled the man with the birdcage.

Wiggle wobble. Oh no! Sukee was shaking herself dry. Dad pulled Tan Tan away as droplets sprayed like rain.

The moment I dismounted, Tan Tan asked again if he could have a ride.

'I said ten dollars!' said Dad.

The man lowered the birdcage to the sand and rooted in his pocket.

'He's only joking,' I said.

'British humour, I suppose,' said Dad, and grinned. 'Come on lad, I'll take you. How about once up and down the beach?'

Dad lifted Tan Tan on to Sukee's back and with a swish of her tail, they were off! The man rushed to catch up with them. He had a limp. Was he Tan Tan's dad? They looked similar.

I was alone. The sun shone bright as a laser. I drank some water, watching Sukee grow smaller and smaller, watching her disappear behind a big boulder at the end of the beach.

When should I tell Ma about her? She would probably say riding was dangerous.

Would she be angry with Dad? I hoped not.

The birdcage was wooden and its cotton cover was stained red. No birdsong. Not even a tweet. Who wants a little bird when you have a pony?

A seabird with yellow legs landed close by. What kind of bird was in the birdcage anyway? Why was it so quiet?

Nobody was looking. I tugged at the zip to take a peek. No tweet. No fluttering of wings. Just notes, paper notes. Piles of them.

I unzipped higher. Yellow notes. Stacked high. Money? *Wa*! Yes! A stash of cash. Thousands upon thousands of Hong Kong dollars!

I looked up, sweat dripping into my eyes. Sukee appeared from the other side of the boulder and Tan Tan waved. Quickly, I zipped the birdcage shut.

'*Ho wan*. That was great,' said Tan Tan. I snuggled my face in Sukee's mane, not daring to look at him.

Shh. I haven't told anyone about the money. Yet.

Chapter 5

My Sad Sad Story

Ma *was* mad about Dad buying me a pony. Ponies were not only dangerous, but dirty, and very expensive to keep.

Grandma Pau Pau shouted too.

I shouted back, refused to eat, then felt bad for being rude and ungrateful. And that night, I had a dream, about birds. They stuffed Ma's money in their beaks and flew into the dark. When they wanted to give the money back they got lost. Ma was very sad.

Like me sometimes, when I think about her and Pau Pau. I can't help it, but I blame myself for what has happened.

You see, I was born with six toes on my right foot. When I was a baby, we all lived in Pau Pau's house in Mui Wo. But then my foot grew wonky and the doctor said I needed operations. Dad says the problem started when Pau Pau wouldn't let me have them. They'd hurt too much, she said.

One night he got really mad and smashed her Buddha. Soon after, we left him and moved to Tin Shui Wai and I was only allowed to visit at weekends. Dad moved nearby, saying he'd keep an eye on Pau Pau's house but she told him not to bother.

And sure enough, as I grew, I could only walk on tiptoes. People pointed and laughed at me. Then I couldn't attend the local primary school because it had stairs. That's when Pau Pau finally agreed to the operations. Not just one. Many.

All I remember of those days is pain, pain, pain. How often had my leg been cased in heavy white plaster, my skin itching like a thousand mosquito bites?

If the latest operation had worked, I should be able to walk normally. Maybe I could start proper school after all. I wouldn't know until the doctors removed all the bandages.

I couldn't wait to find out.

I would either be like everyone else my age, or ... still crippled.

I couldn't bear imagining that.

At least I now had Sukee. Only three more

days until I'd see her again!

First I'd kiss her muzzle and tickle her ears.

Then I'd trace a six-pointed star on her forehead.

Then I'd brush her tail and polish her hooves.

I telephoned Dad to ask how Sukee was. He'd bought her a saddle. She'd become friends with BC. And Ronny had planted some carrots for her.

If Ronny's carrots were ready, I'd give her one as a treat.

Chapter 6
Now You See It, Now You Don't

Tally ho! Off we go. Up Tiger Mountain to look for pink dolphins.

Tally ho! That's what British people say when they want their ponies to go faster. But *whoa!* When Sukee quickened her pace to trot downhill, I nearly fell off.

Some hikers dived off the path for cover.

But soon we were climbing again, Sukee and Dad and me. A soft breeze blew and Dad named the flowers along the way: bauhinias, azaleas, hibiscus. He plucked a wild orchid and clipped it into my hair.

High on hill, we found a comfortable spot overlooking the sea. Dad laid an old bath towel on the grass and I unpacked our goodies – jam sandwiches, tomatoes (a bit squelched), cans of soda, and peanuts. Naughty Sukee rooted for some apples I'd left inside the rucksack.

The sea looked as flat as a Peking duck pancake. Pink dolphins are seriously endangered, Dad said. The new bridge and airport runway would probably finish them off.

How sad. I was munching my apple listening to Dad telling me something about concrete-mixing when something nudged my head.

It was Sukee ... nibbling my orchid!

'She loves you so, she'd eat you too if she could,' said Dad.

I stroked her satin-smooth coat.

We mistook a dolphin for a large chunk of rubbish. I was half-listening to Dad listing other seriously endangered creatures, half-watching the sea, when two motor boats zoomed towards each other, and stopped.

Dad peered through the binoculars, whistled, passed them to me.

Three men were exchanging heavy crates of something at the bows of their speed boats. One man had a limp. Remembering the birdcage, I was about to tell Dad about the money when the boats quickly parted and one roared towards us.

‘Smugglers?’ said Dad. ‘I bet there’s a police boat around.’

Something tingled my spine when a big grey boat, bristly as a brush, appeared from around the headland.

I stood up. ‘Where’s it gone?’ I couldn’t spot the boat that should have been closest to us.

‘Probably hiding in a cove,’ replied Dad.

Sure enough, it reappeared after the police boat had sailed away.

Dad and I talked about smugglers all the way home.

Chapter 7
Discoveries

Mrs. Potts' flowery dress was soaked in sweat and her spring-onion-root hair was screwed in a bun. 'Oh, for a pony,' she said, a metal cage strapped to her back.

She was going to rescue a puppy. What could be more fun? 'I'll ask Dad,' I said. He'd been saying he'd let me ride alone soon.

Mrs. Potts strapped the cage behind Sukee's saddle. Sukee didn't seem to mind. She was much more interested in snatching mouthfuls of grass.

The country park made my heart sing.

Trees swayed in the breeze. The air smelt fresh and green. On the way, Mrs. Potts told me about a deer she'd once rescued from the catchwater. 'Cute as Bambi he was.'

She stopped to check a map. 'The pup was spotted around *here,*' she said.

All *I* could see were bushes, rocks, and distant mountains shimmering in the heat.

Mrs. Potts put the cage on the path, opened the trap door and hooked a straggly piece of beef inside. Then we hid behind a tree.

'*Shh*!' Sukee kept tugging leaves off its branches.

Scuffle. Scuffle. A black pup's head peeked out of a bush. It trotted towards the cage, sniffed. One cautious step forwards, then another, and it was inside the cage!

One bite of the meat and – snap – a lever sprung to life, pinging the door shut. Yelping, the pup ran in circles trying to get out. Mrs. Potts clapped her hands and whooped.

The pup cowered when Mrs. Potts reached inside the cage. Lifting his back end, she told me it was a male.

Right there and then I named him Smudge. 'Because of this little patch of white on his neck,' I said.

'You must come back to my house and name my other orphans,' said 'All fourteen of them.'

Fourteen animals looking for homes! When I'm big, I'll have a big house with a big garden and all abandoned animals can come and live with me.

Croar croar! Cicadas and the sun beating down on my back like toast. From high on horseback, in a wood, I spotted the roof of a solitary old hut. 'Do you think it's a smugglers' den?' I asked, remembering something Dad had told me about their need for secret meeting places.

Mrs. Potts shrugged. 'I dare you to take a look,' she replied, mopping her brow.

I steered Sukee towards the trees, careful to avoid being slapped by low branches. Was it my imagination or was there a fishy smell?

A battered door, barred windows – padlocked, and – a shiver ran up my spine – big black spiders lay like hairy hubs on wheel-sized webs. Inside, stacks of crates, nets, and a rusty motor boat engine.

'Someone's coming!' cried Mrs. Potts. I screamed, Sukee jumped, Smudge barked.

Mrs. Potts burst into laughter, and teased me for being a scaredy-cat all the way home.

Yum! As a thank-you for helping, Mrs.

Potts cut me a slice of her homemade apple pie.

Smudge gobbled up her old mashed potato.

Outside, Sukee snacked on her garden bushes.

'That's my favourite red hibiscus, I'd have you know,' said Mrs Potts.

She was fostering nine dogs and five cats. I couldn't think of names for all of them but she gave me seconds of ice-cream anyway. 'For that foot of yours,' she said.

And that got me worrying a bit. Was it healing? It felt itchier than ever. What if the operation had failed, like last time, when my toes looked as bruised and bloody as a bunch of grapes? I tried to wriggle them and it hurt.

Chapter 8
New School?

'What's up, Twinks?' Dad said. How could he always tell when something was wrong?

We were watering Ronny's vegetable garden while he was working in Kowloon.

I'd just got back from riding, exploring a nearby village, where I'd followed the cries of happy children, and discovered the local school. The playground was as big as a football pitch and classrooms lined a long, single-floor building – my heart bumped. That meant there were no stairs!

Then an idea jumped into my mind which

grew and grew until I couldn't stop thinking about anything else.

'I think my foot is getting better,' I started, wriggling my toes. *(Ow!)* 'But if it doesn't, do you think I could come to school ... in Mui Wo?'

Dad kept hosing. Water pooled. Hadn't he heard what I'd said? My heart sank.

He turned off the water tap and whistled. 'School in Mui Wo? I wonder what that Pau Pau of yours would think about *that*?'

I grabbed my crutch and swung towards him. 'Pleee-se?'

Dad sighed. 'I'll see what I can do.'

I hugged him as tightly as a screw top.

Next minute he told me he'd phoned the principal and arranged an interview. 'But don't tell Ma yet,' he added, which made me feel horrid.

Next morning, I woke up at sunrise and crept past Dad sleeping on the sofa. In the field, I lay down beside a sleeping Sukee, stroked her beancurd muzzle, tickled her nostril with a blade of grass, and told her of my plan.

Her ears twitched.

Birds chattered. I tied Sukee to her pole and brushed off the mud caking her coat.

Fried eggs and salty bacon sizzled. '*She's* not coming too, is she?' Dad called from the kitchen window.

I gave him one of my pleading looks.

Dad clicked his tongue.

Before he changed his mind, I quickly trimmed Sukee's mane and tail with scissors. I ran my hand down the back of her leg, pulled her fetlock, and – *abracadabra!* – she lifted her foot and up and I cleaned her hooves.

It was break-time. The school gate was open so we went inside and Dad tied Sukee's reins to a basketball post. Some children ran over to stroke her. 'Who are you?' a girl asked.

I smiled nervously and reached for my crutches.

Principal Pang had grey hair and kind eyes. He asked me some questions in Cantonese – how old I was, what my favourite subject was. When I said Maths, he asked me twelve times eighteen.

I quickly calculated the answer in my head.

Principal Pang smiled. 'Do you have an English name?' he asked.

I took a deep breath. 'Twinkle is my name and I've always loved stars.'

Principal Pang did a show-your-teeth smile and Dad winked. He looked so funny wearing a tie and proper shoes.

When Principal Pang asked me some more

easy peasy questions in English, my bad leg stopped shaking. 'You are welcome to study here next term, whether on horseback or not,' he said.

Dad slapped his thigh.

There was quite a crowd of kids milling around Sukee. She was swishing her tail and nuzzling their pockets. I couldn't wait to tell her the good news.

'Hi!' said a voice.

It was Tan Tan, smiling. 'When can I have another ride?'

'Ask your dad,' I replied.

Tan Tan looked confused for a moment. 'Oh, that guy was my uncle.'

That night I couldn't sleep for excitement. Please, PLEASE let Ma agree.

Chapter 9

The Limping Lion Dancer

Would my family let me go to school in Mui Wo? Their final decision wagged faster than Smudge's tail. Of course it depended on my foot but I realized that crippled or not, I'd rather go to school there.

'Let's see,' said Ma.

I folded my arms and pouted. 'That means Pau Pau doesn't agree.'

'Hmm,' said Pau Pau, when I asked her myself. She was in the living room lighting incense sticks to pay respects to our ancestors.

'Why do we always have to follow Pau Pau's wishes?' I asked Ma, later.

‘Filial piety,’ said Ma firmly.

Then Pau Pau decided she’d like to live in Mui Wo after all. She’d grown up there and missed the sea and picking papaya.

Meanwhile Ma said the air in the city was even more polluted now, and that she missed Dad sometimes, even though they’d talked about divorce.

But then they both changed their minds again. *Aargh!*

At least there was some good news: an X-ray showed my bones had fused and my cast could be removed the following week.

To celebrate, Dad gave me the money to buy a chestnut cake. The baker came out specially and passed it to me in a red-ribboned cake box.

A crowd had gathered to enjoy a lion dance for the opening of a new book shop. I nudged Sukee towards boys banging gongs and drums.

Three sets of legs jumped and kicked underneath the lively lion’s body. Two men controlled the lion's head, one sitting on the other's shoulders. Somehow they shook the lion's head, blinked its eyes, gobbled packets of *lai see*.

Gobble! Jump! Crash! Bang!

As the lion danced, something caught my attention: the man at the lion's tail had a limp.

Dee-dah, dee-dah! A police van slowed to a stop and two grim-faced policemen jumped out. They pushed through the crowd to the bleeping of walkie-talkies and the clink of handcuffs.

Sukee jerked her head, nearly knocking off the helmet of one of them.

'Control your animal,' said the policeman sternly.

Another police car, flashing blue lights, policemen circling the crowd. 'Get out from under there. You're under arrest,' the old one shouted, grabbing the lion's tail.

The lion froze and the musicians fell silent.

I suddenly remembered the money stuffed in the birdcage and my tongue felt dry. I almost turned Sukee homewards – surely the cake must be melting – but then the man at the tail, followed by a man from the middle, appeared. They were breathing heavily.

I couldn't believe what happened next.

The police arrested a man.

Not the man with the limp. No, not him.

One of them from under the lion's head.

Chapter 10
Seafood Racket and Smudge

The moment the police drove away, everyone was talking about the price of prawns. Lobsters and crabs too. How expensive they'd become because smugglers sold directly to Mainlanders to make more profit.

'Smuggling is usually a family business,' I remembered Dad telling me. My heart sank. I rushed to Tan Tan's house.

No one was home.

Dad was lounging by the vegetable garden drinking beer. 'Let's have a slice of cake then,' he said.

My crutches were propped against the fence in their usual place so I could dismount myself.

Easier said than done with a cake. *Whoops!* It nearly slid out of my hands.

Why hadn't I told Dad about the cash in the birdcage anyway? Was it linked to the arrest at the bookshop too?

When I told him, he rubbed his chin thoughtfully.

We scanned the newspaper the following day: 'SEAFOOD-SMUGGLING LION!' the headline read, and there, in the middle of the page, was a photograph of the hut I'd discovered in the woods!

Mrs. Potts telephoned. 'You said it smelt fishy, didn't you?' she said. 'And by the way, someone is coming to adopt Smudge. If you want to see him one last time, come now.' I quickly saddled Sukee and begged Ronny for some of BC's bones.

Smudge wagged his tail when he saw me.

Gripping a bone between his teeth, he ran into the corner of the kitchen and gnawed it.

The door bell rang, and who should enter but Tan Tan, and the man with the limp. My tummy lurched.

'Will he make a good guard dog?' said the man, following Mrs. Potts into her office.

'Depends if you take the trouble to train him,' said Mrs. Potts.

Tan Tan looked sad. I didn't know what to say to him.

Luckily he talked first. 'I wish he was for me,' he said, tickling Smudge's tummy.

I tickled Smudge's ears. 'Isn't he?'

Tan Tan frowned. 'No, my uncle wants

him.'

My heart was bumping but I just had to ask him. 'And your dad ... is he the one who was arrested?'

Tan Tan's lower lip trembled.

That's when I understood everything. 'You can come to my house and ride Sukee anytime,' I said.

Tan Tan sniffed.

And for some reason, I wanted to cry too.

Chapter 11
A Moo for the Year of the Horse

Yeah! No more operations! No more crutches! No more being laughed at!

My cast was off. The doctors had finally removed it. My leg was pale from being imprisoned for so long, but otherwise looked just like any other girl's.

'... and its butter yellow eyes bored into my soul.' Mrs. Potts' eyes flashed as wildly as the injured fish owl she'd spotted on her dawn nine-abandoned-dog walk. The chocolate cake she'd baked since smelled like heaven. 'Be brave.' she said to me, twisting my right ankle. *Ow!*

Twinkle Toes Tango. That's what Dad called my foot exercises. Ten times clockwise, ten times counter-clockwise. Squeeze and stretch and JERK!

Where was Tan Tan? We'd arranged to meet after my physiotherapy session.

The chocolate cake made my foot feel even better. 'I prefer pink hibiscus anyway,' said Mrs. Potts, gazing out of her window. Sukee had reduced her bush of red ones to a stump.

'Smudge fell in the river,' Tan Tan explained when he eventually turned up. He jumped on Sukee's back and asked if he could try trotting.

I twitched my right foot. It was probably not up to running alongside Sukee, yet. But Sukee knew the way home. 'Grip the saddle,' I said, then '*Tally ho!*' and Tan Tan bounced down the lane like a sack of radishes.

I hobbled happily behind him. In a couple

of weeks I'd be hobbling to school along this lane, dressed in bright white uniform, wearing shiny new shoes.

Unless it rained. Then I'd ride Sukee, like Principal Pang said I could. I even had a new friend – Tan Tan!

Who was back, bursting with something to tell me. 'There's some grown-ups in your dad's home,' he panted.

A delicious smell floated from the kitchen. The smell of happy times of Ma chopping, frying and boiling.

I gasped. There she was! Pau Pau too. And there was Dad, standing behind them, waving.

I blinked away real tears.

'See you. Tomorrow?' said Tan Tan gently, handing me Sukee's reins.

'Come and eat while the food is hot,' called Ma, as if Sukee was invisible. I untacked her and let her loose in the field, where she rolled.

Pau Pau tutted. But I hugged her tightly, British style. Then Ma. 'Pooh, go and change your clothes,' she said.

Were they coming to live in Mui Wo after all? The more I wondered, the faster I dressed.

No more long bus rides! No more days without Sukee! Every weekend we'd rescue dumped pets with Mrs. Potts!

The television blared the Chinese national anthem. *Click click* went our chopsticks as we dug in to pork and *dofu* and chicken and fish.

Suddenly, Dad reached over the table to serve Pau Pau. Ma glanced at him and I quickly looked down at my bowl.

But Pau Pau dipped the dumpling with chilli sauce, and ate it!

Then Dad served Ma the fish's cheeks – her favourite.

I looked up at Ma. Her eyes were bright.

And that's when I knew it!

'It'll be fun to cycle again,' she said.

'My roof is leaking,' said Pau Pau.

'I can fix that in no time,' said Dad.

Whether we'd all live in Pau Pau's house

again, it was too early to say. But my heart sang with hope. Hope that we could and would. Hope that, like Sukee's four legs, we'd stand strong and tall together.

A cow poked her head through the window and moo-ed.

'A moo for the Year of the Horse,' I said. Everyone laughed.

Mooncake Magic: A Modern Chinese Fairy Tale

Chapter 1
Moony and his Double-Duck-Egg Heart

Driiiiing. The oven bell rang in the kitchen. It was time for Cook Chan to take out his batch of traditional mooncakes baked for the Mid-Autumn Moon Festival. He slurped the last of his breakfast noodles, put on his tall baker's hat.

Swish SWISH went his wife's old rattan brush next door. Chan Tai was sweeping the bakery floor. 'You and your Traditionals,' she grumbled.

Cook Chan opened the oven to pastries

puffed warm and sweet and placed them on the hob. 'We would eat you in the park – my mother, my father, my sister and me. We'd gaze at the bright white moon.'

Click CLICK. Chan Tai's head poked through a bamboo bead curtain between the shop and the kitchen. 'At least my Shanghai Pinks sell!' she said.

Chuckling to himself, Cook Chan invented names for his Traditionals: Moony, Red Bean, Nutty and Suzhou Ham.

Ding Ding, seven'o clock, chimed the bakery clock. Cook Chan disappeared behind the kitchen's back door to fetch a delivery of flour, sugar and eggs.

Click, CLICK. Chan Tai pinned back the bamboo bead curtain. Behind her back, over by the shop's display window, Moony saw colourful cakes stirring: buns, custard tarts, chocolate éclairs. On the top shelf, bright pink mooncakes rolled inside a winter wonderland display of icicled trees and snowmen.

Chan Tai entered the kitchen and opened the fridge.

'Me! Me!' cried a gaggle of Shanghai Pinks.

Chan Tai carefully placed some on a plate and carried them to the winter wonderland. As she slid open a glass panel, a blast of chilled air escaped.

Moony shivered. 'She won't put me in there too, will she?' he asked a dusty plastic pie who hung diagonally opposite on the bakery wall.

'No, only her precious Pinks,' answered

Pecan Pie. 'A Traditional like you will last long in normal temperatures. Until you're eaten, that is.'

'Eaten?' Moony's double-duck-egg heart missed a beat. 'Why am I eaten?'

Pecan Pie thought awhile. 'Because you're tasty and nutritious, made as you are with sweet lotus paste and salty duck eggs.'

'Salty duck eggs?' All Moony could see of himself was pastry.

'Two, actually.'

Hidden deep inside himself, Moony felt them beating.

'And because you're shaped like the moon of course,' added Pecan Pie.

The moon? What was that? Moony tipped his body to catch his reflection in his mould. He saw he was round. Very shiny.

'Cook Chan glazed you with beaten egg,' explained Pecan Pie.

'But what's so special about the moon?'

Pecan Pie recited a famous Chinese poem:

Beside my bed in a pool of light
Is it hoarfrost on the ground?
I lift my eyes and see the moon,
I bend my head and think of—

Creak! went the back door. Cook Chan was coming back.

'Don't move, everyone!' called Pecan Pie.

Moony flipped flat.

Chapter 2

The Traditional Gang v. Modern Rivals

Cook Chan lovingly eased his Traditionals out of their moulds while Chan Tai sifted flour and cracked eggs.

'Can I move again?' said Moony, as Cook Chan ditched the moulds in the sink.

'No,' said Pecan Pie. 'If Cook Chan sees you, he may have another funny turn.'

He recounted how Cook Chan once spotted a jam tart visiting a sausage roll. 'The silly man fainted, banged his head on the till and spent three days in hospital. Never been the same since.'

'Oh dear,' said Moony, as the cook lifted the mooncake beside him and placed him onto a tray.

'Red Bean,' said Cook Chan. 'You're the lucky one because you are filled with thick red bean paste.'

'That's because red is a lucky colour, right?' said Red Bean.

Cook Chan didn't answer. Too bad people can't hear cakes talk.

Chan Tai could hear Cook Chan, though. 'Oh do shut up,' she said.

Cook Chan ignored her. 'Nutty.' He raised the mooncake as if it was an offering to the gods. '*You* have five types of nuts inside you.'

'Then I'm as nutty as a fruitcake,' said Nutty.

Cook Chan lowered his voice respectfully 'Suzhou Ham. You are as oily and salty as the South China Sea.'

'Oily and salty? I don't like the sound of that,' said Suzhou Ham.

'Because you're stuffed full of ham,' said Pecan Pie.

'From happy pigs, I hope,' said Suzhou Ham gloomily.

Cook Chan's floury hand reached for Moony. He sniffed him, sighed deeply. 'And Moony,' he said. 'The tastiest, sweetest, saltiest mooncake in the whole wide world.'

Chan Tai banged her mixing bowl against the table. 'That's quite enough nonsense for now.'

Poor Cook Chan! Moony vowed never to shock him.

Nevertheless, the longer he stayed put, the longer he longed to roll to the bakery window. He wanted to see the moon, if only for a quick peek. It sounded such a beautiful, mysterious place.

Ding ding, eight o'clock, chimed the bakery clock. The keys on Cook Chan's belt jangled as he unlocked the front door.

Customers jostled for a space in the queue.

'Gimme a taste of your Shanghai Pinks,' said a man, elbowing an old woman out of the way.

Two younger women pushed him aside. 'We were first!'

Shaped like Shanghai dumplings, the Pinks had jelly bodies, pink-iced coatings and twisty topknot hair. Chan Tai lifted one from the winter wonderland display, laid it on the counter and reached for a knife.

The Shanghai Pink twisted and twirled her hair.

Moony gasped. What was happening?

Chop, CHOP! Chan Tai's sharp knife flashed silver as she chopped the Pink into pieces.

'Disgusting!' cried Moony.

'Delicious!' cooed the customers.

'She's outta luck,' said Red Bean.

'No pain no gain,' joked Nutty.

'Death comes to us all,' muttered Suzhou Ham.

Chan Tai ringed the cash register and the Shanghai Pinks cheered at the clink of coins in the till.

A flake of Moony's pastry broke off. He already knew he would be eaten, but he hadn't expected it to be so ... so brutal.

'In the olden days, when people were hungry, they would save their mooncakes until the festival,' said Pecan Pie.

'What festival is that?' asked Moony.

'The Moon Festival, when Hong Kong people used to buy pretty red lanterns, picnic at a park and marvel at the moon.'

'Until the parks were paved with concrete,' said Suzhou Ham.

'But I want to see the moon before then,' cried Moony.

A gaggle of giggling Pinks responded:

'No chance of that!'

'You might not even make it to a park.'

'The weather is far too unpredictable these days.'

'You'll be eaten inside buildings, as a snack.'

'Inside offices, washed down with fizzy drinks.'

'In flats while children play computer games.'

Moony's double-duck-egg heart pounded. 'You don't care, about not seeing the moon?'

Laughter rippled around the winter wonderland:

'Not a crumb.'

'Not a cherry.'

'Not a chestnut.'

'We're not sentimental Traditionals, like you.'

One thing was for sure. Moony cared.

And if he was to be chopped and eaten any time soon, he'd tip and roll to see the moon ... that very night.

Chapter 3
Moonstruck

The clock chimed midnight. There was a flapping of moths around a bare light bulb and a scuffling behind concrete walls. Chan Tai was still in the kitchen preparing a new batch of Shanghai Pinks. *Monstrous mooncakes,* thought Moony. *She's never going to finish and I'm never going to see the moon.*

'Don't worry,' said Pecan Pie. 'You're a Traditional, and there are still a few traditional people who like to celebrate outside.'

The moment Chan Tai turned off the lights and headed to bed, the cakes started moving.

'Follow me!' said Moony to his traditional friends. He tipped on his side and rolled along a draining board towards a hatch in the wall. It led to the back counter and the display window.

Nutty and Red Bean spun speedily behind him.

'Wait for me!' puffed Suzhou Ham.

Moony came to rest beside the winter wonderland on the top shelf. Nutty and Red Bean flopped beside him.

'Rolling will be the death of me,' said Suzhou Ham.

Moony's double-duck-egg heart beat strongly as he gazed up into the night sky. A thick layer of cloud lay across it like a dirty old kitchen towel. Where was the moon?

'That's smog,' said Pecan Pie.

'Ssshh!' said the Shanghai Pinks. 'You're disturbing our beauty sleep.'

Smog? Moony lowered his gaze to the street's flashing neon lights. Tall buildings – so many of them! – piled on top of each another like layered sponge cakes.

'The moon has run out of shine,' said Nutty.

'It's there somewhere, right?' said Moony.

'Doubt it,' said Suzhou Ham.

'Let's hope so,' said Pecan Pie. 'Because the moon festival is the night after next.'

The night after next sounded like a long, long wait, and the longer Moony waited, the more the tall buildings seemed to crowd above him, making him feel small and unimportant.

'Do you want to hear a joke?' said Nutty.

Suzhou Ham groaned.

When is the moon not hungry?
When it's full.

Moony *thought* he got the joke. 'Full, like...?'

'Like on the night of the Moon Festival,' said Pecan Pie.

'Except you won't see it because that smog won't clear up in time.' said Suzhou Ham.

'No, no. We're in luck,' said Red Bean excitedly.

Moony followed his friend's gaze. High above, a huge creature ducked and dived between the high-rises. With a flick of its tail and a flap of its giant red wings, it blew the smog away.

'The fair weather dragon!' whooped Pecan Pie.

As the sky cleared, Moony saw bright, light twinkling points. Stars.

And then, he saw the moon. The glorious moon. Rounder and shinier than any Traditional. Cooler and brighter than any Shanghai Pink.

Moony's double-duck-egg heart glowed with pride.

Chapter 4

The Moon Goddess

The mooncakes basked under the moon's silvery beams while Pecan Pie told them the legend about a goddess who lived there.

'Chang'e was sent as a punishment for stealing from her husband, Hou Yi, a famous archer. In ancient times, ten suns shone on earth and people were dying of heat. Hou Yi shot nine of them down, and the heavenly emperor was so pleased, he rewarded him with a magical potion of everlasting life. Hou Yi gave the potion to Chang'e for safekeeping but one night a goddess came to ask for it back and

Chang'e drank it. When the heavenly emperor found out, he was so angry he banished Chang'e to the moon, where she has lived ever since.'

Moony looked skyward, and shivered. The moon suddenly seemed cold, aloof, a very faraway place. 'Isn't Chang'e a bit lonely up there?'

'Not with Jade Rabbit to keep her company,' said Pecan Pie.

'I hope she likes carrots,' joked Nutty.

'I'm sure she prefers mooncakes,' Red Bean.

'Especially the one picked by the moon fairies on the night of the Moon Festival,' said Pecan Pie.

Moon fairies? Who picked a mooncake for Chang'e? Moony stared in wonder as Pecan nodded his pie. He boasted that he'd spotted them flying down from the moon in a chariot every year around this time. The fairies were tiny things, with filo-pastry-thin wings. Like butterflies, they only lived for a day or two.

Moony gazed at the starry sky and his big heart glowed with hope. Not only had he seen the moon but maybe he could go there too. He watched the moon playfully slip in and out of passing clouds. For a moment, he thought he spotted a moon fairy. *Please, oh please pick me,* he whispered.

Meanwhile, the Pinks were excitedly spinning and twisting in their icy world. 'The fairies are sure to pick me. I'm so pretty!' squealed one.

Moony flipped over to his Traditional friends. 'If Chang'e is a goddess, surely they'll pick a Traditional, like us?'

Deep into the night, he and his friends put their pastry heads together to discuss.

Chapter 5
A Cake-in-the-face Affair

The winter wonderland sparkled, and two Shanghai Pinks burst out of a side door and propped it open. Others bounced out and massed on the shelf, circling the Traditionals.

'Hey, what's wrong with you?' said Moony.

'What's wrong with *you?* Don't you know what time it is?' said a Pink.

'Anyway, *we're* all sugar and ice, and all things nice, why would the moon fairies pick you?' said another.

'Because Cook Chan says we taste better,' said Moony fiercely.

'Hear, hear,' said the Traditionals.

'You really believe that?' a particularly podgy Shanghai Pink shouted, 'Destroy them!' She hurled herself at Moony.

A flurry of Shanghai Pinks fell like snowballs on top of the Traditionals.

Bish, bash, slam, splash. It was a real cake-in-the-face affair, until—

'Stop moving!' called Pecan Pie. Someone was coming downstairs.

It was Cook Chan. The cakes froze.

Ding ding, five o'clock, chimed the bakery clock.

Cook Chan walked into the kitchen and poured himself a glass of water. Behind his back, the Shanghai Pinks sneaked back into their winter wonderland.

But the Traditionals had come from the kitchen. They eyed each other, wondering what to do. Moony really didn't want to cause the cook another funny turn. Through the bamboo curtain, he watched him boiling his breakfast noodles.

'Now!' called Pecan Pie, as soon as Cook Chan went out of the back door.

The mooncakes spun as fast as they could, through the hatch, along the kitchen top, until – oh no! – Chan Tai was coming downstairs. She entered the kitchen and tied a frilly apron around her moony middle.

'Me, me!' called some Shanghai Pinks as Chan Tai opened the fridge door.

'Quick!' said Moony, rolling back to the hob.

Creak! The back door opened. The mooncakes ground to a halt near the sink. They were still a good foot away from their tray.

'We're done for,' said Suzhou Ham.

Cook Chan dug into his noodles with his chopsticks. He went towards the sink to rinse the bowl.

Eiya! What were his mooncakes doing piled up, over *there*?

'Anything wrong?' asked his wife.

'No, no,' said Cook Chan, and straightened

his tall baker's hat. 'In fact, hey! I've got an idea, a money-making idea, for my Traditionals.'

'Yes?'

Cook Chan picked up Nutty, smelt him, smoothed a flake of pastry. 'I'm going to package them together. Create an ... assortment,' he said.

'Assortment?' snorted Chan Tai.

'Yes. A *special* assortment, for *special* people.'

'That doesn't include me, I suppose?'

Cook Chan wiped some flour off his chin. 'Maybe not.'

Chan Tai shook her old rattan brush. 'You and your Traditionals,' she said.

Cook Chan lifted a tin out of a cupboard and dusted it. On its lid, Moony saw a colourful moon festival harvest scene with ancient people tethering bullocks, lighting lanterns, exchanging cakes, laughing, praying.

But his double-duck-egg heart sank deeper in his lotus paste. If he was put in that tin, how would the moon fairies find him? When would he see the moon again?

'Nice knowing you!' called Nutty, as Cook Chan lowered him inside.

Chapter 6
Tinned

Stuck in the tin, placed one shelf below the winter wonderland, the Traditionals argued about what could be worse than being stuck in a dark stuffy tin one shelf below a winter wonderland.

'Never seeing the moon again,' said Moony.

'Moony, you are traditional with a capital T,' teased Red Bean.

'Well, what's yours?' said Moony.

'Not being able to flirt with those pretty Shanghai Pinks,' Red Bean replied.

'Being stuck in a sewage pipe,' decided Nutty.

Suzhou Ham laughed, for once. 'But that's where we'll all probably end up.'

Moony wriggled unhappily in his crinkly curved casing. It wasn't being eaten that bothered him. It was those chattering Shanghai Pinks. Their shrill excited voices were driving him crazy. From time to time, there would be a banging and thudding as they bounced on the tin. His lotus paste boiled at the thought of them being picked by the moon fairies rather than a Traditional.

'I never believed in that fairy nonsense anyway,' said Suzhou Ham.

'I did,' said Moony.

'I did too,' said Red Bean.

Nutty offered to tell some jokes:

What do you call a tic on the moon?
A luna-tic.

'Ha ha, that's funny,' said Red Bean.

Suzhou Ham moaned.

'He's only trying to cheer us up,' said Moony crossly. 'Next one, Nutty.'

Nutty cleared his throat.

Did you hear about Chang'e's
party on the moon?
Her mooncake was delicious
but there was no atmosphere.

'I bet that mooncake was a Shanghai Pink,' said Red Bean. 'They're all so sweet. Maybe pink is the new lucky red.'

'Oh do be quiet,' said Suzhou Ham.

Nutty lost his cool. 'I'm not feeling nuts about being shut up with you either,' he snapped.

'Oh dear. The sooner we all get eaten up, the better,' muttered Suzhou Ham.

Then Moony couldn't stand the bickering anymore. 'Let me out of here,' he cried. With all his strength, he jumped.

Hurrah! He landed outside the casing. He tipped and rolled towards the tin wall, gathering speed, and slammed into it.

The tin moved, very slightly.

Moony's double-duck-egg heart tripped a beat. 'Copy me, friends,' he cried.

Red Bean and Nutty jumped out of their casing too. They tipped and rolled towards Moony. It took Meaty Suzhou Ham a few attempts but his brawn was just what they needed.

'One-two-THREE!' they shouted as the tin swayed back and forth, each time tipping some more.

Could the mooncakes jiggle it so as to tip it off the shelf?

Chapter 7
Be Careful What You Wish For

Crash! The mooncake tin landed, flipping off the lid, spilling the Traditionals across the bakery floor.

'Oh, rats' tails. They're back!' said a Shanghai Pink.

She bounced back into the winter wonderland to tell her friends.

Moony quickly rolled up to the winter wonderland shelf. Red Bean, Nutty and Suzhou Ham followed hot behind him.

'Watch where you're going,' complained a Swiss roll as they spun past her.

‘Have the moon fairies been?’ Moony asked a Black Forest.

The chocolate cake shook its cherries.

‘Maybe we’re still in luck!’ said Red Bean.

‘Yes, you may be,’ called Pecan Pie. ‘The official celebrations won’t start until tomorrow evening.’

Moony looked out of the window. Strung along the lampposts, there were rows and rows of red lanterns dancing in the night breeze. Strung along the street, people carried bagfuls of cakes.

But the sky was blanketed. Except for a wispy cloud, which drifted lazily across a distant mountain range. Was it the moon fairies’ chariot? His double-duck-egg heart thudded.

But it wasn’t. Moony sighed.

‘Be careful what you wish for,’ warned Pecan Pie. ‘It’s said that Chang’e rules the moon like a tyrant. When she has a bad temper, she rages like a storm. She can shoot satellites out

of the sky, blow aeroplanes off course, push people down waterfalls.'

Why is she so angry? Moony wondered.

'You must be joking,' said Nutty.

Pecan Pie frowned. 'I've heard that Chang'e recently whipped up a tsunami. She tossed and tumbled thousands of people into a massive wave, half-drowned them. Then she blew the wave away and laughed at the people squirming.'

'I hope the moon fairies don't choose me,' said Suzhou Ham.

Moony shivered. Chang'e did sound a bit scary. Did he *really* want to be picked? He looked up at the sky.

As if to banish Moony's gloomy thoughts, the fair-weather dragon swooped down through the smog. With a whip of its tail and a flip of its wings, it batted the blanket away. And there, light and shiny, was the bright white moon.

Moony whispered a few lines of a beautiful ancient poem Pecan Pie had taught him:

I long to fly on the wind
Yet dread those crystal towers,
those courts of jade
Freezing to death among those
icy heights.
Instead I rise to dance with my
pale shadow
Better off, after all, in the world
of men.

Chapter 8
Attack!

Moony's friends joined him marvelling at the moon. It shone like a gigantic silver dish, offering the mooncakes a taste of the magic to come.

The clock chimed midnight. It was Mid-Autumn Festival day. The day the moon fairies were sure to visit.

Behind them, a group of Shanghai Pinks bounced out a hole in the skirting board and slyly slid back into their winter wonderland.

From the hole Moony heard a scrabble, scrabble, scratch, scratch – rats! Small fat furry ones. Long thin skinny ones. All twitchy noses and whiskers. A small fat furry one scaled up the shelves, coming straight for him.

'Go away!!' he cried, as the rat raced towards him, snapping its razor-sharp teeth.

The rat lunged at him and they fell off the shelf together.

'Ha ha!' laughed the Shanghai Pinks.

Red Bean dive-bombed from the shelf to the floor, landing on Moony but knocking the rat out cold.

'Jump back into the tin!' shouted Pecan Pie.

Moony jumped.

As did Red Bean.

But Nutty and Suzhou Ham, as if frozen in fear, stayed rooted to the top shelf.

From the safety of the tin, Moony and Red Bean watched, horrified, as more rats scrambled up the poles to surround their friends. 'The meaty one is mine,' squeaked the fattest one.

Suzhou Ham tipped and rolled, but was easily caught by the rat, who bit him to pieces, chunk by chunk. His insides hung like stringy sausages from the rat's mouth.

Another rat gripped Nutty in its paws. Peanuts, almonds, walnuts, pumpkin and sesame seeds rained off the shelf. 'It doesn't hurt,' said Nutty.

'Roll away!' cried Moony.

Crash! Moony left his words behind as a rat hurled itself at the tin.

The tin shot across the tiles and smashed into the wall.

I'm finished, thought Moony as two paws scrabbled against the lip. The rat eyed him hungrily.

But then there were footsteps, from above. Approaching fast.

It was Chan Tai, in her nightgown and slippers. 'Cook Chan, come here!' she called, panting. She clutched the counter to catch her breath.

Cook Chan stood behind the bamboo bead curtain, and covered his eyes. 'I daren't look,' he said.

'Oh, don't be such a baby,' said Chan Tai.

Cook Chan's face appeared. He pulled at a long mole hair on his chin.

'Ugh, rat droppings,' said Chan Tai who'd noticed some slimy brown things on the floor.

She walked into the kitchen, returned with her old rattan brush and a large black bin bag. 'I think we should chuck the lot,' she said.

'No, no!' cried Moony as the mouth of the bin bag gaped open.

Cook Chan lifted the tin off the floor and tipped it.

Red Bean plopped inside the bag.

But Moony fell on to the tiles. 'I got away!' he cried, tipping and rolling back to the kitchen.

'Aaagh!' cried Cook Chan. 'Did you see that?'

Thud! He'd fainted.

Swish, SWISH! Moony flew towards blackness.

Chan Tai had swept him into the bin bag. With Red Bean and some super squashed Shanghai Pinks who'd got caught up in the brawl.

Chapter 9
Close Encounters

Chan Tai threw the black bin bag on top of the rubbish piled on the street. *Ow!* Moony hit the pavement with a THUMP.

Remarkably, despite the battle with the Shanghai Pinks, he was still in great shape.

Red Bean looked okay too. 'I can't believe I'm still alive!' he said, emerging from a cluster of bun wrappers.

Suzhou Ham definitely wasn't. Just a few scraps of fat remained of him. For all his doom and gloom, Moony would miss him.

Nutty wasn't alive either. He'd morphed

into sprinkles of half-eaten nuts. For all his nuttiness, he'd been such fun.

But for some reason, Moony's sad thoughts didn't last for long. 'Let's escape from this smelly bin bag,' he said.

They rolled and rolled. They pushed and pushed. But – monstrous mooncakes! – the bin bag seemed to be tied at the top.

And the city was waking up. Taxis honked, trams screeched. *Ding ding, eight o'clock* chimed the bakery clock, as people crowded into Chan's bakery.

Shake, SHAKE! What was happening? Moony was bounced around the bin bag like popping corn.

'Help!' cried Red Bean.

Something strong and smelly was pummelling them.

'Get off me!' cried Moony.

The stray dog ripped the bag open with frantic paws. His wet nose skimmed past the mooncakes as he sniffed out old bones.

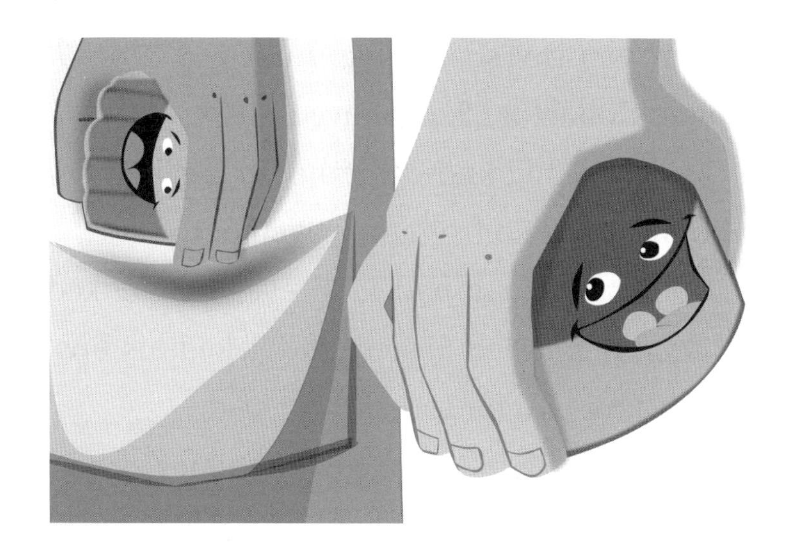

Quickly, Moony and Red Bean wriggled towards the light and dropped to the pavement.

'Shoo!' called a man from a noisy, orange, metal machine parked on the nearby kerb. Stacked with newspapers, plastic bottles and lunch boxes, its shelves were moving, crunching, grinding.

'This way,' called Moony, as the rubbish collector leapt out of the cab and shooed the dog away.

The mooncakes rolled and rolled but weren't fast enough. 'What have we here?' said the man, taking off his gloves.

'Did you say something, Collector Wong?' shouted Collector Chan above the din.

Moony didn't know whether to laugh or cry as he was plucked from the pavement.

Collector Wong had kind eyes but looked hungry. He fondled Moony and licked his lips. 'But I'll save you for tonight.' he said.

Red Bean hadn't managed to roll far either. Collector Wong easily caught him. He showed him to Collector Chan. 'Do you have someone special to give this to?' he asked.

Collector Chan stopped throwing bin bags into the chomping mouth of the machine for a moment. 'Thanks, big brother. Red Bean mooncakes are my daughter's favourite,' he replied.

Beep, BEEP! 'Get a move on, lads,' shouted the driver from the cab.

'I'm in luck,' called Red Bean as he disappeared into Collector Chan's pocket.

'Goodbye, dear friend,' called Moony.

Just before being popped into a pocket too.

Chapter 10

A Magical Celebration

That night, Collector Wong took his family to a park to celebrate the Mid-Autumn Moon Festival in a traditional way.

Snug in a picnic hamper, Moony heard waves slapping against sea walls, bamboo flutes playing, poetry being read.

He was laid on a tablecloth with pomelos, grapes, Asian pears. And one other mooncake. She was undersized, delicate, and smelled sweetly of egg. Moony hadn't seen one quite like her.

'What's your name?' he asked.

The mooncake pouted.

'I'm a Traditional,' said Moony.

'And I'm from an expensive hotel in Kowloon,' said Miss Peninsula, and turned her pastry on him.

Oh well, he was only trying to be friendly. Moony tried not to let it bother him. After all, time was short and there were so many other lovely things to see.

Like the silvery shadows playing on soft grass.

Like the merry lanterns swaying from trees, their warm golden flames flickering against the night sky.

Moony inhaled the sweet scent of freshly baked steamed buns, the melting wax of candle forests happy children were planting around him. Collector Wong's children, he supposed. Their grandparents, wrapped as tightly as sausage rolls, sipped piping hot tea.

Moony's double-duck-egg heart glowed.

Scattered around the park, other family

members circled mats under the bright white moon too.

'Moony?' called a familiar voice. It was Red Bean! Collector Chan was picnicking on a bank nearby. Beside him, a pale-faced girl, Collector Chan's daughter, Moony supposed. Where was the girl's mother? Moony didn't understand why she wouldn't be there.

'At least my luck only needs to be split into two,' said Red Bean.

Collector Wong's daughter raised her chin, closed her eyes and sent silent wishes up, up, up into the sky. 'Where do they go?' she asked.

'To Chang'e, the moon goddess,' said her mother.

'Will she send her blessing back to me?'

'Oh yes,' said Wong Tai, and gave a tight-lipped smile.

Then Collector Wong's son also lifted his face to the moon. Blinking in its bright light, he silently mouthed a long sequence of words.

'That was a long one,' said his sister.

‘I told Chang’e a secret,’ the boy said.

‘What is it?’ teased his grandmother, and began to sing a song.

A breeze soft as whipped cream floated across Moony’s pastry. He imagined the boy’s secret as a cloud scudding along the silvery path of moonlight that lay across the sea. The water looked as smooth as icing.

How I wish all my friends were here to see all this, he thought.

Grandmother finished her song and everyone applauded. Collector Wong stood up, stretched, and reached for Moony.

Moony’s heart thumped.

Who wants a slice of mooncake?’ said the collector.

Oh no, this is it! Moony closed his eyes. He’d already prepared what to do at that moment. *What a happy little life I’ve had,* he started. *Thank you my friends for sharing it with me. And thank you, fair weather dragon, for clearing the sky whenever I wanted to see the moon. And thank—*

'Aaaagh!' cried the posh Peninsula. Moony took a deep breath to calm his beating double-duck-egg heart and clenched his eyes shut.

Warm eggy breaths filled the cool air and everybody was praising the mooncake's flavour. He snuck a look at sweet lotus paste swirling on tongues, salty yellow yokes smearing teeth. Maybe there was something beautiful about being eaten after all.

'More!' cried the children.

Moony clenched his eyes shut again, continued his thanks. *Thank you, Pecan Pie, for being so helpful. And thank you, my dear Cook Chan, for making me.*

The breeze gathered its strength and shivered the leaves of the tree, which rocked the lanterns like babies' cradles, and cast magical shadows on the grass.

There was a swish of butterfly wings. Thousands of butterflies' wings.

No, it was the swoop of bats.

Or was it?

Moony opened his eyes, and blinked. In front of him were tiny joyful faces, twinkling lights, a dainty chariot.

The moon fairies! A flock of them, dancing around him. The forest of candles flickered and flamed.

'Who's blowing the candles out?' said Collector Chan's daughter as the moon fairies swept Moony into the chariot, whisked him up to the crown of the tree.

The lanterns swung gently below.

'He's a beauty,' said the fairy queen, brushing her butterfly wings across Moony's face.

'Can I see?' cried a fairy.

'Later, later,' said Asparas.

The moon fairies' voices tinkled like bells and the chariot creaked as they entwined Moony in their silvery threads.

'You want ... me?' said Moony.

Laughing merrily, the fairies swirled and twirled themselves around the silken ropes of the chariot roof. Its silk-spun wheels whirled as they sang a Happy Mid-Autumn festival song to anyone who was listening.

Collector Chan's daughter heard them. She would never forget the enchanting melody.

Then suddenly, the chariot rose, as if fired by a magnetic force.

'Aren't you the lucky one?' someone called.

Red Bean.

'Oh goodbye, my dearest friend,' called Moony. A mixture of sweet and salty feelings churned inside him as he looked down. He was

already higher than the highest sponge cake buildings. And the lanterns below twinkled like an upside-down heaven of colourful stars.

With a lurch, the chariot whooshed towards the silver sea, towards the shimmering path of moonlight that sparkled ahead.

Chapter 11
Another Mean Trick?

A shower of cosmic dust streamed behind the chariot as the moon fairies rocketed Moony to Chang'e. Moony's salty feelings turned sweet as they flew past shooting stars, sonic comets, glittering galaxies.

The moon fairies taught him the Chinese names of the constellations – White Tiger, Red Bird, Black Tortoise, Blue Dragon – and clapped their butterfly wings whenever Moony answered correctly.

'Are you sure Chang'e wants *me*?' said Moony. He still couldn't believe he'd been chosen.

'Of course. She's a goddess and you're a Traditional. I wouldn't make the same mistake twice,' said Asparas.

The moon fairies burst into laughter.

'What mistake?' asked Moony.

Haha! The fairies collapsed in a heap of laughter around him. 'Ask Jade Rabbit,' said one, snatching a breath.

So it was true! Chang'e really did have a rabbit to keep her company.

'Thump, thump,' said Moony, pretending he had legs.

Hahaha! The fairies twisted and twirled in their silken gowns.

At first, everything seemed such fun.

But when the tip of fair weather dragon's tail disappeared behind earth's dark side and didn't re-emerge, Moony began to feel nervous. Earth had shrunk to a ball and the desolate white orb that loomed ahead made him feel empty inside.

Be careful what you wish for, he remembered Pecan Pie saying, and a chill cooled his double-duck-egg heart.

A strange humming sound that had accompanied them along the journey grew louder and louder the closer they came to the moon. Moony's head began to ache with worry.

'It's the sound of people's wishes, millions and millions of them,' a fairy said.

Oh for hands to cover my ears. Moony thought. The noise was deafening now. *For hands to cover my eyes.* The land that ranged ahead had bumps and crevices.

Then the chariot keeled. Brakes shrieked. *Weren't they landing too fast?*

They landed in a storm of moon dust. It rained down on Moony like icing sugar. Like the angry Shanghai Pinks, Moony thought, hard, cold, but white.

He coughed and spluttered. Was this another mean trick planned by them? Had they somehow arranged for him to be banished to this giant winter wonderland?

In the distance, atop a mountain, the icy turrets of a palace loomed tall.

Chang'e's palace, a moon fairy told him.

Moony shuddered. 'I don't like it here,' he said.

The fairy looked confused. 'Wasn't this your dearest wish?'

Moony tried to sort his thoughts into some kind of shape.

To see the moon? Yes. But to be on it? No!

To be chosen by you? Yes, once. Until I heard about Chang'e's stormy temper. Then, I wasn't so sure.

'Please take me back to earth,' he said.

'Too late,' cried the moon fairies, flapping their butterfly wings, brushing Moony free of moon dust.

Swish, swish. The moon fairies flapped themselves into a perfect revolving circle above Moony.

'Onward!' cried Asparas.

Like a swirling bouquet of blossoming flowers, the moon fairies opened their wings and swooped down, smothering him.

'Let me out,' Moony cried. He couldn't see a thing.

He felt himself lifted on to the familiar hardness of the chariot seat.

Then, *whoosh!* He was whisked through the cool clear air.

Chapter 12
Wu Gang the Tree Chopper

Whish! The chariot wheels skimmed across the land, and slowed. 'One, two, *three!*' said Asparas, and the moon fairies shook their wings and released their captive.

Moony, dizzy and confused, gathered his senses on the soft mattress of their feathery gowns.

Then, remembering where he was, tipped and rolled towards the lip of the chariot, and stopped.

It was no use trying to escape. Where could he roll to?

A cool wind whistled down from the mountain above. Moony followed the contours of its flanks. And there, at the top, he spied Chang'e's palace again. It looked like a giant white heavily decorated mooncake. There were windows and doors but all seemed bolted. Oh well, at least he would meet a goddess.

'I'll make my own way, thank you,' he said stiffly and flipped off the chariot.

Tittering behind him, pulling the chariot with silken threads attached to the base of their butterfly wings, the moon fairies followed.

The climb seemed surprisingly easy, even

though Moony was rolling uphill. But as he climbed he became aware of a curious banging. It grew louder and louder, echoing around the icy mountain range, pounding against Moony's double-duck-egg heart.

In the distance, someone was chopping a tree – its leaves were the only green in a sea of whiteness. The person was dwarfed by a mound of torn branches. 'Is that Chang'e?' said Moony.

Hahahahahaha. The moon fairies rolled around the chariot clutching their tummies with laughter.

Ah, it's a man, thought Moony, as he saw the person had a big bushy beard.

'It's not funny,' said Asparas.

Moony turned to press on, when there was a flurry of wings and the moon fairies swooped down to pick him up.

'What are you doing?' said Moony angrily.

Rats' tails. He was back in the chariot, swaddled underneath a wardrobe of fairy gowns.

'Well met, Wu Gang,' called Asparas.

The chopping had stopped. 'No, wait,' said Wu Gang.

'Keep going, fairies,' said Asparas.

Clomp! Wu Gang's great boot formed a boulder on the track and the chariot shuddered to a halt. 'Not often I can enjoy the smell of a mooncake,' the man said.

Who was this strange man? Moony popped his head between the fairy gowns. 'It's only me,' he said cheerfully.

Wu Gang strode towards him.

But Moony was admiring the tree that arched above him. 'What a splendid tree,' he said, when – *creak!* – a new branch sprouted from the trunk. How odd!

And where did that monstrous pile of dead wood come from?

'Keep away,' shouted Asparas.

Wu Gang was so close to Moony that a tuft of his nostril hairs brushed against him.

'Attack!' shouted Asparas, and the moon

fairies flapped their butterfly wings in Wu Gang's eyes.

Wu Gang licked his fat rubbery lips. 'But the mooncake is talking to me,' he said.

Moony's heart skipped a beat. 'Er, I was saying what a beautiful tree you have. Why ever are you destroying it?'

'Aaah!' Wu Gang's hoary breath showered moon dust as he collapsed in a heap of self misery. 'If only you knew my story.'

'What story?' said Moony. Pecan Pie had only told him about Chang'e. He had no idea a hairy man lived on the moon too.

'There's no more time,' said Asparas firmly. 'Jade Rabbit is waiting for us.'

Ah, Jade Rabbit, Moony thought, he'll be able to tell me.

Wu Gang looked at Asparas with doleful eyes. 'I can't even have a lick of him? I mean, it's not as if there's a big clock ticking here, and whether or not—'

Asparas smacked his mouth with her wings.

'How dare you say that, on the only day when time really matters. Chang'e *must* have her mooncake before the night is out.'

As the fairy spoke, Moony felt the chariot soften beneath him. Its silken threads seemed to be losing their mysterious lustre.

Bang! Wu Gang took a swipe at Moony, nearly knocking him out of the chariot.

'Onward!' commanded Asparas, and the chariot lurched forward as she gave a string of orders.

Moony watched as a swarm of moon fairies swarmed around Wu Gang's face.

'You can at least tell me a little bit about him,' said Moony.

Asparas didn't answer.

The tree was sprouting branches again. 'Chopping that tree is some kind of punishment, isn't it?' said Moony. 'What did he do wrong?'

Swinging above him on a silken rope, Asparas paused for breath. 'Wu Gang was an impatient mortal who became a god. But even as an immortal he kept making short cuts, so the heavenly emperor sent him here where he has to chop that tree for eternity.'

'Unless the emperor gives him a second chance?' said Moony.

Asparas frowned.

Immortal. Mortal. God. Man. Moony was muddled. 'Immortals are gods who live in heaven, right?'

Asparas nodded.

'But people are only mortal, which means they can't go to heaven until they die, unless they have a magic potion that can make them live forever, like Chang'e.'

The moon fairy straightened her diamond crown.

Asparas was mad at him but Moony's double-duck-egg heart flickered with hope. 'Do you think Chang'e has a drop of that magic potion left for me?' he said.

Asparas couldn't help laughing. 'I don't think it would work on mooncakes.'

Moony looked back. Poor old Wu Gang had picked up his axe and was hacking at the laurel tree again. 'Keep chopping,' he called.

'If only it were so simple,' said Asparas, as the chariot gathered speed and – *whoosh!* – Moony felt himself hurled through the air again.

Chapter 13
Has Chang'e Changed?

Moony found himself on the top of a silver cake stand surrounded by shelves of cups and saucers, plates and jugs. It reminded him of Cook Chan's kitchen, which saddened him for a moment. What a long way he had travelled since then.

'Well met,' said what looked like a giant fluffy-tailed rat with big ears: Jade Rabbit, Moony supposed. But Jade Rabbit was not at all how he had imagined. He was tall as a child, and stood upright with his ears pinned back to the collar of a jade suit. The suit stuck to his

body like green icing. And one of his legs was a bony stump.

'Good work, moon fairies, a Traditional,' Jade Rabbit said.

'*Hahaha*. We learned our lesson last time,' said the moon fairies, busily flying around obeying Asparas's orders. They dusted the porcelain, opened biscuit tins, arranged sweetmeats around Moony's cake stand, which took pride of place on a trolley. A sweet smell of freshly baked cakes filled the air. It seemed there was going to be some kind of party.

A tea party, a moon snap told him.

Moony flipped flat. 'I don't mind so much about being eaten, but—'

'What's the matter then?' snapped the moon snap.

'Temper temper!' called a moonberry pie from the shelf below.

Steam poured from a kettle spout. 'Boiling,' whistled the kettle.

Jade Rabbit sprinkled some dried petals into a waiting tea pot, doused them with water, and limped back to a chair, where he checked his pocket watch. The clock had three hands and Chinese-looking squiggles on its face.

'Two *fen* and I'm done,' said the teapot.

Moony wondered what the teapot was saying but it seemed like an opportune moment. 'Why did the moon fairies pick me?' he asked.

Jade Rabbit twitched his nose. 'Let's say that last year's didn't go down too well.'

'I don't quite understand,' said Moony.

Jade Rabbit stretched his good leg. 'Let's

say it didn't go down at all.'

Moony felt more confused. 'Do you mean...?'

'Don't push me now,' said Jade Rabbit. 'I don't want to give you hope. Neither do I want rumours to spread. There's been far too many of those.' He took a little brush out of another pocket and brushed his bony stump.

'What happened, to your leg?' asked Moony.

'Oh do, do do tell him. I love that story,' said the teapot.

Jade Rabbit twirled his whiskers as if undecided. Then his body jerked and he stared at Moony with beady eyes. 'Promise you won't tell anybody?'

Moony laughed. 'Whom can I tell? I mean, all my friends are eaten and, unless there's something you haven't told me, or something I haven't understood, I will soon—'

Jade Rabbit raised a paw.

'Do tell,' said the teapot. 'After all, he's going to—'

The Jade Rabbit stamped his stump and the teapot huffed a puff of steam.

What was going on? Moony laughed nervously.

Jade Rabbit caught his eye. 'Okay, I'll tell you all you need to know,' he said. 'You've probably heard that the heavenly emperor sent me to the moon to keep Chang'e company.'

Moony nodded.

'And that she almost immediately set me to work grinding medicinal pills and pellets in a pestle and mortar, in the hope that I could make another elixir of life for Hou Yi.'

Moony nodded again, although he hadn't heard that part of the story.

Jade Rabbit lowered his head solemnly. 'But the elixir wasn't needed because Hou Yi died, was killed actually. He floated up to heaven, where he has stayed ever since. Imagine Chang'e's anger when she realised that they could never be together again. I raced around the moon, desperate to find things to make her feel better. I offered her some of my own fur to cushion her throne, but she always burnt it, until recently. I asked fair-weather dragon to deliver the finest teas in China but she wouldn't drink them. Once, I served them in the best eggshell porcelain, but she smashed the lot.'

Moony gasped.

'That's when I decided to give her a slice of my suit, even though it had moulded to my leg many years ago.' Jade Rabbit patted his good leg, as if to make sure it was still there. 'I presented the jade ring as a bangle, and, miraculously, Chang'e was so pleased with it, her anger softened. So, despite the bad things people say about her, I vouch that Chang'e has changed.'

Jade Rabbit reached for a knife and tapped his good leg with it. 'And this one's next.'

Moony gulped as the blade of Chan Tai's knife flashed through his memory.

Suddenly the moon fairies were flocking

around him, singing a merry song:

Peace on earth
Peace on the moon
Peace to all who
Hear this tune.

But Moony didn't feel peaceful at all.

Chapter 14
Not Even a Piece of Crater Cake

While Jade Rabbit stacked cups and saucers, jugs and plates beneath him, Moony introduced himself to the selection of icy white cakes neatly displayed around him on the cake stand: moon snaps, lunar pies, silver drops.

'Pleased to meet you,' they replied icily.

Jade Rabbit placed the teapot on a lower shelf and gave his suit a final polish. 'Time to tune your instruments, moon fairies,' he said.

The fairies flew off.

'Hold tight,' said Jade Rabbit, wheeling the

loaded trolley towards Chang'e's icy chamber. A cold air chilled Moony's double-duck-egg heart.

Oh, so what. I'll be eaten and that will be that, he thought grimly.

But his double-duck-egg heart pounded at the first glimpse of Chang'e. Reclining on her rabbit-fur throne, she wore a magnificent white gown and her hair was as long and black as the night. She was wafer thin, almost ghostly. A flock of fairies massed on a stage playing strange beautiful music for her, but she was gazing wistfully at the distant stars.

'M'lady,' said Jade Rabbit, and bowed.

Chang'e swept back some stray hairs from her face, and murmured, 'Oh, is it time for tea?'

Moony's fear melted. She didn't seem storm-like at all.

Chang'e leaned towards the trolley. *Jangle jangle,* her jade bangles slid down her elegant arm and Moony gazed into the two black moons that were her eyes. 'Ah, a Traditional,' she said.

'Fresh from Hong Kong,' said Jade Rabbit.

Chang'e sighed. *Jangle, jangle* went her bangles as she lay back on her rabbit fur throne. 'I'm not hungry,' she said.

Moony was confused. At first she'd seemed so interested in him. Now her head was turned and she was staring back into space. Had this happened before? The conversation between Jade Rabbit and the teapot began to make sense.

Chang'e would eat nothing else, either. Not even a piece of crater cake.

Jade Rabbit's whiskers twitched. 'Play

some music,' he ordered the moon fairies, and they plucked their zithers and blew their bamboo flutes.

'Did she want a Shanghai Pink after all?' whispered Moony to a silver drop.

Chang'e overheard and laughed unkindly. 'Not if they're anything like the sickly sweet novelty I was offered last year. Once was quite enough. What was it called again?

'Snowskin,' called Asparas from the stage.

Hahahaha giggled the moon fairies.

'Quiet!' said Chang'e.

And I won't say another word, thought Moony.

Jade Rabbit edged closer to Chang'e. 'Even if you don't eat *anything,* you know your beautiful body won't waste away,' he said.

Chang'e blinked away a tear. 'Who would believe that everlasting life was such a curse.'

Jade Rabbit kneeled beside Chang'e's throne and rested a paw on her lap. 'Now remember m'lady,' he said. 'Whoever we are, immortal or mortal, goddess or man, we all have to bear the burden of living forever.'

Chang'e moaned. 'Remind me why,' she said.

The fairy's music faded into the background but Jade Rabbit's beady eyes shone brightly. 'Because we all have spirits inside us, and our spirits *do* live forever. The only difference between you and man is that man dies because his body grows old.'

'Oh, to be mortal again,' sighed Chang'e.

Moony's double-duck-egg heart warmed. Chang'e didn't seem angry. Just very sad.

Chapter 15
The Ultimate Sacrifice

But then Chang'e flew into a terrible rage. 'If we all live forever, why doesn't Hou Yi come to visit me?' she cried.

'Oh dear, oh dear,' said Jade Rabbit.

Chang'e turned to Moony. 'Tell me, why, little mooncake.'

'Be-because you stole his magical potion?' he answered.

Chang'e howled. 'You see? Even he has heard the nasty rumours about me.'

'Nothing like a cup of tea to soothe the nerves,' said Jade Rabbit.

But Chang'e's eyes hadn't left Moony's. 'Let me tell you, little mooncake, that is *not* the reason.'

The moon fairies played their music louder and Jade Rabbit placed a porcelain cup on a saucer. 'If only Hou Yi knew how miserable you are without him,' he said gently.

'I did *not* steal his potion,' said Chang'e, between gritted teeth. 'A goddess tried to steal it from *me*. She came down to earth to take it back because Hou Yi hadn't drunk it.'

'I believe you,' said Moony.

But Chang'e wasn't listening. 'And when she commanded me to hand it back to her, I drank it. Why? Because I panicked. Who wouldn't, if threatened by instant death? That goddess was powerful.'

'I'm sure,' said Moony.

Chang'e laughed scornfully. 'And how could I have guessed that the heavenly emperor would punish me by banishing me here?'

'Calm down now, m'lady,' said Jade Rabbit.

But Chang'e's eyes were flashing green. 'You want to know why Hou Yi doesn't visit me?'

'Oh y-yes,' said Moony.

Rising from her throne, circling high above, her gown billowing in a gathering wind, Chang'e screamed, 'Because he's forgotten me, that's why.'

The moon fairies plucked and blew their instruments still louder but the wind whirled stronger and a strange humming grew.

A chill stole across Moony's heart.

'He used to love me so much, and I loved him,' she wailed. 'I didn't drink the potion because I was jealous of his fame, or because I was fed up with spending so much time home alone. No no no! Those are just evil rumours spread by envious people. It was *his* idea to choose a special day to drink the potion and share it, half each. So that the two of us could live together forever. That's how much he loved me.'

Chang'e spiralled wider and longer. Her angry movements broke into zigzags that spiked the air.

'Come down!' cried Jade Rabbit.

The flash of a knife, a gleam of jade. Moony swung round, to see Jade Rabbit, eyes clenched, his knife poised to slice another piece of jade from his leg.

'Please don't!' cried Moony. He couldn't bear the pain.

The wind ebbed and subsided. Chang'e

flopped back on her throne. 'Yes, Jade Rabbit, that's enough. I've told you before. You have suffered *enough*,' she said. 'We have all suffered enough.'

Tears rolled down her cracked cheeks.

Why was she so unhappy? Moony didn't understand. But how he wished he could make her feel better.

Sighing, Jade Rabbit pocketed his knife and poured Chang'e a cup of tea.

The fairies' music softened into something sweet and smoothing.

Then Moony knew what he could do. His double-duck-egg heart felt lighter, free.

He tipped upright, rolled from the plate to the edge of the trolley edge, and jumped on to Change's lap. 'Eat me,' he said.

Chang'e raised her head. She smiled. She looked so beautiful when she smiled.

Jade Rabbit stood holding the teapot, rooted to the spot, as if re-living a distant memory.

Chang'e lifted Moony up, placed him on her palm, examined him. Her lips were red and her teeth sparkled. 'Why should I?' she said.

Moony flinched. He'd have to give a reason. Like Pecan Pie always did. 'Because I'm a Traditional?' he said.

Chang'e smiled again. Her flushed pink cheeks fired his confidence. 'And why deprive yourself the pleasure of eating me?' he said.

Chang'e cupped Moony in her warm hands and looked at him curiously.

Chapter 16
A Short Little Life that Wasn't in Vain

As Chang'e bit into Moony, her eyes moistened. 'The smell of your delicious filling reminds me of cooking lotus flower seeds with my grandma,' she said. 'We'd wash and boil them, peel the shells. Add sugar cane and stir, stir, stir. And I'd beg to lick the spoon.'

'Have another bite,' urged Moony.

Chang'e's shiny white teeth dug into him but her tongue was smooth and moist. 'Then I'd bend bamboo beside a crackling fire,' she said, 'make lanterns with my grandpa and papa.'

'And what was your favourite animal?' asked Jade Rabbit.

'Mmm, now let me try to remember,' she said playfully.

Tweaking his whiskers, Jade Rabbit refilled her cup. The fragrance of jasmine leaves and the moon fairies' music warmed the cool air.

Moony enjoyed the feeling of his lotus paste slipping down Chang'e's throat.

She asked, 'Do children still shell seeds with the grandmamas? Make lanterns with their papas?'

'Oh yes,' said Moony, although he wasn't entirely sure.

So he quickly changed the subject and talked about best friends instead: Nutty the joker, sweet Red Bean and grisly Suzhou Ham.

He made her laugh at the sickly Shanghai Pinks.

She drew him closer when he told her about the happy children he'd left in the park sending her their dearest wishes.

'Ah,' she said, leaning back into her furry throne. 'At least the children haven't forgotten me. I always do my best to bless each and every one of them. I'm sure *they* would forgive me if they knew my true story.'

As she spoke, the vast blackness seemed to still. Stars twinkled.

Moony was beginning to feel faint. He forced himself to focus. *Forgive. Forgive.* What bothered him about that word?

'Ooh,' said Chang'e, scooping his paste with an elegant fingernail. 'You have a double-duck-egg heart.'

Then Moony knew what he wanted to say. His words came out fragmented. 'One for Hou Yi ... and one for you,' he said weakly.

Chang'e tensed. The moon fairies, sensing her sudden change of mood, played louder.

Jade Rabbit jumped to attention. 'Do try the Oolong, m'lady,' he said, reaching for another teapot.

But at that moment, Moony knew his short

little life hadn't been in vain and his big double-duck-egg heart beat deep. Because Chang'e was smoothing more of his lotus paste on her tongue, accepting the offer of more tea.

'Before the sun comes up, how about you ask the moon fairies to fly us to heaven?' he whispered. 'There, you can share my double-duck-egg heart with him and ask for his forgiveness.'

Chang'e brought Moony's double-duck-egg heart to her lips. She kissed him, nestled him to her chest. 'You, little mooncake, are the wisest little sweetmeat I've ever met,' she murmured.

As if by magic, the cups and saucers, cake stand and cakes collected themselves together and flew back to the kitchen. Jade Rabbit's stump vanished and he was two-legged again.

Asparas started shouting orders and the moon fairies put down their instruments, flocked around the chariot, tightening its silvery ropes, spinning its silvery wheels.

Moony felt so faint he could barely speak. ‘And while we’re there, how about we ask the heavenly emperor for his forgiveness too?’

Chang’e threw her arms to the sky, as if a terrible weight had been lifted from her. ‘To heaven’s gate,’ ‘To gate!’ she cried.

She swept Moony up into her gown, swooped to the chariot and they all flew off into the night sky together.